Pretty Boy Detective Club

The Swindler, the Vanishing Man, and the Pretty Boys

By NISIOISIN

Translated by Winifred Bird

VERTICAL.

Pretty Boy Detective Club
The Swindler, the Vanishing Man, and the Pretty Boys

Editor: Daniel Joseph

PETENSHI TO KUUKIOTOKO TO BISHOUNEN

© 2015 NISIOISIN

First published in Japan in 2015
by Kodansha Ltd., Tokyo.

Publication rights for this English edition
arranged through Kodansha Ltd., Tokyo.

Published by Vertical, an imprint of
Kodansha USA Publishing LLC, 2020

ISBN 978-1-949980-87-5

Manufactured in the United States of America

First Edition

Kodansha USA Publishing LLC
451 Park Avenue South, 7th Floor
New York, NY 10016
www.readvertical.com

Pretty Boy Detective Club

The Swindler,
the Vanishing Man,
and the Pretty Boys

PRETTY BOY
DETECTIVE CLUB

NAGAHIRO
SAKIGUCHI

MICHIRU
FUKUROI

HYOTA
ASHIKAGA

MAYUMI
DOJIMA

MANABU
SOTOIN

SOSAKU
YUBIWA

Illustration Kinako, Cover Design Veia

Rules of the Pretty Boy Detective Club

1. Be pretty.
2. Be a boy.
3. Be a detective.

0. Foreword

"Heaven does not create one person above or below another." Neither this famous quote nor its famous author, Yukichi Fukuzawa, needs any introduction, but the fact of the matter is that Fukuzawa never wrote anything of the kind. Well, technically he did, but that was not at all his main point.

If you open to the first page of *An Encouragement of Learning* (yes, the equivalent of the very same page you're currently reading in this book), you will indeed find those words printed on the first line, but what he has actually written is: "Heaven does not create one person above or below another, *it is said*," after which he goes on to raise the question of why, despite this fact, the real world isn't like that at all. In short, he argues that education widens the gap between people who start out as equals, so basically his point is, "If you want to be better than other people, then study"—which makes sense, given that his book is called *An Encouragement of Learning*.

But this lesson (which most people prefer not to face up to) has been totally ignored, and only the pleasant-sounding bit at the beginning has been picked up and passed down to future generations. Probably some well-intentioned but imprudent and slightly hasty egalitarian got hold of Fukuzawa's book, and far from following his "encouragement" to actually learn from it, stopped at the first line, which must have been extremely vexing for the great author.

I'd been convinced that cherry-picking a few words from someone else's writing, twisting them around to suit your own interests, and using them however you please was a thoroughly modern technique for the dissemination of information, but apparently it's been a standard strategy of the human race for ages. Of course, if a certain delinquent master of satire heard me say that, he'd probably offer this rebuttal:

"Idiot, it's only thanks to the profusion of that kind of cherry-picking that we can get away with a non-apology like, 'I didn't mean it that way, sorry if my words caused some kind of misunderstanding.'"

And then, he'd probably say this:

"What, you think you've figured out the essence of human nature or something? Aren't you the one who started out by using that famous Yukichi Fukuzawa quote to expound on your pet theory? Stop acting like some kind of opinion columnist already."

Dear oh dear.

But satire aside, he's got a right to his opinion, even if he doesn't have a column for it, and I'll agree with him about one thing—who the hell am I to hold forth on the ways of the world?

So I'll hurry up and get on with the story.

After all, a girl whose only claim to fame is her eyesight should keep her mouth shut unless she really knows her subject, which in my case means sticking to that delinquent master of satire and his compatriots in the Pretty Boy Detective Club.

But if you'll allow me one small clarification, I didn't quote Yukichi Fukuzawa to intimidate anyone—I did it because the story I'm about to tell concerns some pieces of paper bearing the likeness of none other than the famous author himself.

1. You Dropped Something

On that morning, the now fourteen-year-old Mayumi Dojima was walking toward Yubiwa Academy, the private school she attends, in order to pursue her studies just as she had when she was still thirteen years old. If I had to point to one difference between this Mayumi Dojima and the Mayumi Dojima of those first thirteen years, it would be that until recently, she (which is to say I) wore skirts, but now she was wearing slacks.

To put it bluntly, the fourteen-year-old Mayumi Dojima was a girl, but she was wearing a boy's uniform—not that she has a thing for dressing up as a boy, but if that's what people think, so be it. Sorry if my outfit has caused some kind of misunderstanding.

On the other hand, I'd rather people misinterpret my motivations than figure out that I'm wearing a boy's uniform so I can be part of the notorious Pretty Boy Detective Club, that shadowy organization operating behind the scenes at our school.

If you just can't live without knowing the details of how all this came about, then I suggest you read the previous case file (*Pretty Boy Detective Club: The Dark Star that Shines for You Alone*). I'll admit I was afraid that if I dressed like this people would give me even weirder looks than they had before, further reducing my already scant stock of friends, but surprisingly, that hasn't happened.

In fact, it's been the opposite—classmates I had no connection with up till now have started talking to me. Of course, part of it is probably the entertainment value of a girl dressed up as a guy, but I don't think that's the whole story.

The world is tolerant of eccentrics.

Surprisingly so.

Or maybe it's just that Yubiwa Academy is the kind of place that lets "people like that" do as they please to begin with.

It's a...unique environment, shall we say.

...What was my deal, anyway?

I spent all that time staring up at the sky by myself, afraid of changing but equally afraid of being treated like a changeling—but was all that struggle, all that warped thinking, just one big ego trip?

When I think about it, it all seems so pointless, but I'd like to believe that thought itself is the result of having roused myself and braved the first step forward.

Anyway, the fashion sense of the newly fourteen-year-old Mayumi Dojima may have changed a bit, but as she headed toward school, her personality was as grossly twisted as ever—and then.

A businessman walking up ahead of me suddenly caught my eye—needless to say, I was wearing my custom-made glasses at the time.

Glasses that restrict my vision rather than improve it—which means I didn't see him with my "too-good" eyes. I just plain saw him.

I don't know why this businessman on his way to work—this supposed symbol of a peaceful society—caught my attention, but he did.

I'm not suggesting I had some kind of premonition, nor am I getting too big for my britches and insisting I have a natural talent for detective work now that I belong to the Pretty Boy Detective Club or whatever.

But something about him caught my eye.

If I had to say, maybe it was the slightly unnatural way he wore his suit? With his briefcase in hand and his hair slicked back, he was the perfect image of a businessman, at least from the back, but something about him still struck me as ever so slightly off.

Still, the feeling was so faint that if he'd just kept walking, we probably would have passed each other without incident. So faint that five minutes after we'd passed each other I would have forgotten all about it.

After all, life is made up of such fleeting encounters—

yeah right, like I'm really going to start writing enlightened crap like that.

Anyway.

Having this vaguely "off" businessman in my field of vision was making me uncomfortable, so I decided to speed up and pass him—which should have been easy even for a fourteen-year-old, if I took big steps.

And since I wasn't wearing a skirt, it wouldn't be improper. I'd probably even look like a jaunty young man. I hoped.

But just when I'd made up my mind, Mr. Businessman leisurely withdrew a cell phone from his jacket pocket.

Was he calling a client or something?

This early in the morning?

Man, Japanese businessmen have it rough.

But I didn't have time to fully sympathize—because when Mr. Businessman took out his phone, something else fluttered to the ground.

The object seemed to have gotten caught on his phone and slipped out of his pocket along with it—but since he started talking right away, he didn't notice.

Actually, it didn't "flutter."

It thumped.

"Ermph!" I sputtered before I could stop myself. Naturally, I was watching all this unfold with "regular" vision, but for a second I wondered if something had gone haywire with my glasses.

Was this even possible?

Mr. Businessman had dropped a wad of cash.

A bare wad of cash had fallen out of the pocket of his coat—with the paper band still around it, like it was fresh from the bank.

And it was composed of ten-thousand-yen notes.

The ones with Yukichi Fukuzawa's face on them.

In other words, Mr. Businessman had dropped a million yen right in front of me—and to make matters worse, he just kept on striding along, talking on the phone, not noticing a thing.

"W-Wait!"

In a panic, I started running after him.

I'll never forget the way I scooped up that bundle of cash from the asphalt like a seasoned rugby player.

Of course, I'm not a particularly good person, and my moral compass is nothing to brag about—I like to think I have enough class to resist picking up money and sticking it straight into my own pocket, but I also know myself well enough to realize that I'm not so conscientious as to deliver every single lost item I find to the police.

But this was a lot of money. Too much money.

I'm not so emotionally stunted that I'd stand passively by as someone drops a million yen—so I kicked myself into action and managed to catch up with the surprisingly speedy businessman.

"Hello?" I said, like I was answering the phone or something.

The person placing the call obviously shouldn't be saying that, but Mr. Businessman finished up his own conversation just at that moment—and when he turned around, I saw that he was much younger than I'd imagined.

His slicked-back hair made him look grown-up, yet there was something, I don't know, childlike in his eyes.

He definitely didn't look formidable enough to be walking around with a million yen in his jacket—and come to think of it, not even the presidents of major corporations walk around with a million yen sticking out of their pockets.

Okay, slow down.

Get a hold of yourself.

I'd reacted reflexively in the face of that big pile of cash, but what kind of person drops a million yen in the street?

A sketchy person, right?

In a sense, the money had dazzled me into acting rashly, but could Mr. Businessman be—

"Well, well. Whatever is the matter?" he asked in an exceedingly gentlemanly tone, accompanied by an exceedingly gentlemanly smile—and at least for the moment, that gentle smile reassured me.

Though not so much that I actually managed to calm

down.

"U-Umm... You, you d-dropped this," I stammered, holding out the bundle of cash.

"Goodness me, I did?" Mr. Businessman replied, winking at me.

He had a sort of "my bad" look on his face, but at the same time he was a little adulty for that (to use the current slang), so it wasn't exactly charming.

That childlike first impression must have been a figment of my imagination.

"How very careless of me! Thank you. You've done me a real favor, young man."

My heart skipped a beat at the words "young man."

I didn't have the stage presence to say, "I'm not a young man, I'm a pretty boy"—so I mumbled something like, "Oh, um, you're welcome," and handed him the bundle that was weighing so heavy in my hands.

Mission accomplished, I began to feel vaguely self-conscious, so I muttered, "Well, anyway…" and was getting ready to make my escape—when he called out, "Just a moment," foiling my getaway.

"Please, young man, don't vanish so beautifully without at least allowing me to give you a token of my thanks."

"A t-token of your thanks?"

Go ahead and ask me not to vanish beautifully all you want, but it's against club rules to depart awkwardly, so...

"The going rate for returning a lost item is ten percent

of its value, I believe."

"T-Ten percent?" I parroted again like an idiot.

With a practiced hand—a hand practiced at handling bills—Mr. Businessman extracted exactly ten ten-thousand-yen notes from the million-yen bundle and slipped them into the breast pocket of my uniform. The gesture was as crisp as if he were punching a timecard.

Ten ten-thousand-yen notes?

Which is to say, a hundred thousand yen?

A hundred thousand yen, like one of those hundred-thousand-yen coins that are worth a hundred thousand yen?

"I-I can't take this, I mean, I would never accept a reward for what I did, I don't need it, in fact, this puts me in a difficult position, please take it back."

My frantic protests were too late, however—by the time I looked up from my breast pocket, Mr. Businessman had already turned and started walking away.

Hey, come on!

It was me, not him, who ended up put out by a beautiful vanishing act. I ran after him in consternation. This was no joke—somehow, I had to return that money.

"Please, wait! Hey!"

He sped around the corner, and I followed close on his heels, only to be thrown into consternation once again—What the...?

Logically speaking, I couldn't have lost sight of him

because the street in front of me was long and straight, with no side streets to turn down for quite a ways—in fact, I'd been relieved when he turned that corner—but nevertheless, the vaguely unsettling form of Mr. Business-man was nowhere to be seen.

He had disappeared.

Not so much beautifully as completely, unsettling aura and all—like a puff of air.

"Huh? Wha...?"

2. In the Art Room After School

The encounter was so hazy that I wondered if I'd simply been daydreaming at daybreak, but evidence to the contrary remained in the form of the hundred-thousand-yen reward in my pocket.

No matter how many times I looked, it was still a hundred thousand yen.

No matter how many times I counted, it was still a hundred thousand yen.

Crap.

What the hell was I supposed to do now?

I mean, of course it's not only the custom but the law to give a finder's fee of ten percent (Lost Goods Law, Article 4. Strictly speaking, the fee must be between five and twenty percent of the value of the found item), so you could say I had a legitimate right to the money.

Which meant that one option was to gratefully accept it—I could make my very own "my bad" face, giggle "tee-hee, lucky me ♪," and take myself shopping at the mall.

But I'm not that type of person.

I'm not the type to go shopping at the mall, not the type to make "my bad" faces, and not the type to consider myself lucky.

That kind of good luck would screw up my life.

Selfish logic dictated that I couldn't keep the money.

So I wanted to find some way to return it—which meant I had to find that businessman who had vanished so suddenly.

And who better than a bunch of detectives to search for a missing person?

…To tell the truth, I didn't really think I could count on them, but I didn't have anywhere else to turn—so after school, I headed to the art room.

The art room.

That fabulously redecorated classroom where the Pretty Boy Detective Club was headquartered.

The room had sat unused for years after electives were cut from the curriculum, until "those guys" commandeered it and turned it into their private stomping grounds.

"How do you do," I called as I pushed open the door, using the theatrical salutation which had somehow become my habit—and there, in that extraordinary classroom which I never seemed to get used to, with its sparkling chandeliers, magnificent sculptures, stunning paintings, and luxurious carpets, were three members of the notorious Pretty Boy Detective Club, sitting on the sofa sipping tea—it was as if I'd opened the door and stepped into Merry Old England.

By the way, the three members in question were:

Michiru the Epicure, he of the beautiful palate.

Hyota the Adonis, he of the beautiful legs.

Nagahiro the Orator, he of the beautiful voice.

Put the other way around, neither the president nor the child genius was present—actually, since everyone in the club is something of a free spirit, getting all five (six if you include me) in the same place at the same time is more the exception than the rule.

In other words, my first visit to the art room had in fact been a fluke—though we'll set aside the question of whether it was a rare stroke of good luck or an unparalleled misfortune.

"Hey, nice timing—I just brewed this," announced Michiru the Epicure—that is, Michiru Fukuroi, year 2, class A—as he turned toward me. "And don't worry, you'll be able to drink it. I made it shitty enough to suit your underdeveloped sensibilities."

Talking trash from the get go.

Still, it was surprising to hear that he'd specially adjusted his recipe for me without even knowing whether I'd show up.

And speaking of surprising, the fact that the very same "bossman" who inspired terror throughout our

23

school was not only preparing tea for his friends but baking cookies to go along with it was plenty surprising to start with.

"That pretty boy look is really starting to suit you, Doji. As the former mascot of the Pretty Boy Detective Club, I'm insane with jealousy," joked Hyota the Adonis—that is, Hyota Ashikaga, year 1, class A—from his spot directly across from me. Honestly, though, I was the one being driven insane with jealousy.

He was sitting upside-down on the sofa with his legs draped over the back, wearing a uniform he'd revamped even more dramatically than the delinquent sitting next to him, such that the slacks were now short shorts.

His exposed legs shone with a brilliance so legendary it had driven every girl at Yubiwa Middle to start wearing black stockings—of course, the light emanating from the legs of this boy who was both Pretty Boy Detective and ace member of the track team was by no means a skin-deep scam; to tell the truth, despite his angelic adorableness, his real role in the organization had more to do with physical labor than any kind of mascot business.

"Ms. Dojima, has something happened?" asked Nagahiro Sakiguchi, year 3, class A, in his enchanting voice. It was such a lovely voice, in fact, that if I hadn't known the age of his fiancée, even a warped character like me would have long since fallen under its spell.

After all, this was the pretty boy who had risen to

the position of student council president solely on the strength of his speech at the first-year entrance ceremony—although, since he'd just quietly detected that I'd come to the art room for some specific reason, he definitely had more to offer as student council president than just pretty speeches.

Since I was a member of the Pretty Boy Detective Club myself, at least on paper, I was perfectly entitled to come to the art room without a specific reason, but to be frank, I couldn't help feeling hesitant as a newbie—and the student council president seemed to have picked up on that fumbling-in-the-dark feeling. If I hadn't known about his fiancée, I would have been impressed—he definitely deserved his role as vice president of the club.

"Don't tell me you're gonna ask us to do some detective work! What the hell, you're a member yourself now and you're still coming to us with cases? I'll tell you right now, we don't offer an employee discount."

With that abusive tirade, the delinquent graciously placed a cup of tea before me.

Judging from the way he treated me like a proper member instead of keeping me at arm's length like the rookie I am, he must have a really strong sense of team spirit—you could pass that off as typical juvenile delinquent gang mentality, but if you ask me, he's not such a bad guy at the bottom of it all.

He's dangerous, though, don't get me wrong.

…But why was he talking about a member discount? I thought the Pretty Boy Detective Club was supposed to be a pro bono, not-for-profit organization.

"It's about that, right? The bulge in your chest pocket?" Mr. Bare-Legs asked, pointing at my jacket from his upside-down position on the sofa—with his foot, since his arms were crossed behind his head.

The strange thing was that even though pointing with one's foot is clearly poor etiquette, having that gorgeous leg pointed at me felt like the height of courtesy. I guess you could say I'd fallen head-over-heels for his heels-over-head way of sitting.

The folded-up hundred thousand yen was indeed tucked into my chest pocket—right where Mr. Businessman had left it. That was a dangerous place to keep so much money, but I'd been reluctant to put it in my wallet, even temporarily.

I suppose I should have praised him for being so observant, as befits a member of our club—but I couldn't shake the suspicion that he was looking at the bulge of my chest, not the bulge in my chest pocket.

I wouldn't be surprised if he was more interested in how I dealt with my breasts when I dressed as a guy than he was in the case I'd brought—as if I'd ever tell him.

Anyway, I timidly pulled the ten bills in question out of my pocket and placed them on the table.

I have to admit, the luster of that hundred thousand

yen was dimmed a bit by such opulent surroundings...

"Hanh?"

"Would ya look at that."

"Oh my."

Each of the three members responded in his own way.

Unlike me, those composed eccentrics didn't fall apart at the sight of the cash, but they did seem to share my confusion as to the meaning of the money that had materialized so suddenly before them.

And here I was about to tell them a story that involved a sum ten times greater—a million yen. Even this room couldn't make that amount of cash seem paltry.

So, sipping the tea the delinquent had blended just for me, which apparently was called Mayumi No.6 (I wish he'd quit it with the weird names), I revealed the strange events that had befallen me that morning.

3. Councilman, Bossman, and Bare-Legs

"I must say, that's quite the strange story," Sakiguchi observed when I had finished my account—and as far as I could tell from their expressions, the delinquent and Mr. Bare-Legs agreed.

"Right?" I was relieved to have finally been able to share my troubles with someone, but apparently my relief was premature.

Well, "premature" might be an overstatement, but while I was mostly worried about what to do about the hundred thousand yen, the three of them seemed more perplexed by the man who had disappeared so suddenly down that long, straight road.

"A person who vanishes into thin air... That's just the kind of enigma our leader is so fond of. Perhaps we should try our hand at solving this little mystery."

"Can't know till we ask him. Sometimes the president's aesthetic sense is beyond me."

"Sometimes? More like all the time. But I've gotta

admit, I'm hooked. If this guy really did dash off after he turned that corner, I've got an urge to try my beautiful legs against his."

…Well, either way, if they were all interested, I couldn't ask for anything more—if they found Mr. Businessman for me, I'd be thrilled.

I might be ignoring the rules of the Pretty Boy Detective Club, but as long as I could return the hundred thousand yen, I wasn't going to get hung up on beauty.

The fact is, they called themselves a detective club, but I wasn't sure how good these Pretty Boy Detectives actually were at finding missing people—they couldn't be planning to call up a helicopter like last time and search for him from the skies, could they?

"Can you describe the person who dropped the money?"

Whether he sensed my incessant fretting or not, Sakiguchi at least asked a reasonable question.

I answered haltingly—the events that followed my initial glimpse of Mr. Businessman had made such a strong impression that I wasn't very confident in my description of him.

But after I finished, Sakiguchi remained silent.

"…"

And that wasn't all.

"Hmm? Nagahiro, what's wrong?" Mr. Bare-Legs asked, only to be shushed by the councilman.

What was going on? Why wouldn't Sakiguchi even entertain his question? I glanced reflexively at the delinquent, but he was just sitting there looking grumpy.

"Uh, um…? Sakiguchi?"

"Ah, pardon me. It's nothing."

Judging by his overt reaction, it could hardly be nothing, but I didn't feel up to pressing him after he had dismissed it in his perfect student council president speechifying voice.

Considering my position, what I really would have liked to ask was, "Do you know this man?" but…

"What we really must focus on now is what to do with the money."

I couldn't help being swept along by that oh-so-persuasive voice as it nudged the conversation in the very direction I wanted it to go; I'm just going to go ahead and say it—is it possible his vocal cords have the power to brainwash people?

When I considered the possibility that he may have stolen his fiancée's heart in just such a way, I had an urge to bolt right then and there.

"If we're going to approach the matter diligently, then I suppose the most appropriate thing would be to turn the cash over to the police. Even if we never find the man, or if we do find him but he refuses to take the money back, we can at least entrust the money to their keeping."

"I hate the police…"

Hyota the Adonis quietly shook his head.

The solemn, gloomy look on his face was hardly fitting for the boy they called an angel-among-men—did this kid have a bad history with the cops or something? Given his heroic experience of being kidnapped on three separate occasions, I wouldn't be surprised by anything he told me at this point.

"Leaving aside what happened last time," the delinquent chimed in, "a bunch of guys who call ourselves detectives letting the police take care of us at the drop of a hat sure as hell isn't going to do much for our reputation."

In fact, Fukuroi had old acquaintances in the police department (though according to him, they were more unsavory-but-inescapable connections from his delinquent days than "acquaintances"—see the previous case file to find out "what happened last time"), so calling them in would've been easy enough if we'd wanted to, but apparently he had enough backbone to nix the idea of actually doing it.

Or maybe he was just being considerate toward a younger club member who hated the police.

Whatever his motivation, when the delinquent talked about someone "taking care" of you, it took on a whole different meaning.

"It's also true that even if we did take the money to a police box, I doubt they would believe a preposterous tale about a businessman dropping a million yen. They might even think we were mocking them, and give us a good tongue-lashing."

"If that was all they did, we'd be getting off easy..."

Mr. Bare-Legs' bare legs were shaking like leaves.

Honestly, what happened to him?

"Which means our only option is to find this man ourselves. If he appeared to be commuting to work, then the standard approach would be to lie in wait for him in the same place at the same time tomorrow. Ms. Dojima, you said it happened on your way to school—have you encountered this businessman before, then?" Sakiguchi asked.

It was precisely the question I would have liked to ask *him*.

"No, this was the first time. But you're right—if he was on his way to work, then he ought to be there at the same time every day..."

If we both kept a regular schedule, then it wouldn't have been unusual for me to see him every day, yet I hadn't seen him once in the entire year and a half or so since I'd started attending Yubiwa Academy.

Of course, it was possible that I simply hadn't noticed him because up till now I had always been looking up at the sky while I walked...

"If he really was on his way to work, that is," the delinquent interjected. "Any way you slice it, walking around with a million yen in your pocket is pretty fishy."

It certainly is.

I'd thought the same thing myself—his gentlemanly demeanor afterward had muddled the impression somewhat, but my original questions about who exactly this guy was hadn't exactly gone away.

It seemed best to tread carefully where he was concerned, whether we were returning the money or what.

The saying "wise men don't court danger" darted through my mind—and I wondered if perhaps the best approach would be to simply pretend it had never happened.

But if that was to be my conclusion, I should have arrived at it before coming to the art room—because just then, the furthest person in the world from a "wise man" threw open the door I'd just closed, with force enough to nearly tear it from its hinges.

"Ah ha ha ha! Ahem! So you're all here, lads! And shining beautifully, I see, as the esteemed rules of our club demand!"

Not a wise man but a pretty boy.

Manabu the Aesthete, lover of beauty and president of the Pretty Boy Detective Club—which is to say, Manabu Sotoin—had arrived.

4. The President and the Child Genius

The president delivered this energetic speech at the same time he flung the door open, and as I was wondering what he would have done if no one had been inside, I glanced over and saw that he wasn't alone: Sosaku the Artiste, creator of beauty—aka Sosaku Yubiwa, year 1, class A—was hanging back behind him.

As his name suggests, Yubiwa is the scion of the family that runs the Yubiwa Foundation, which in turn runs our school (and what's more, he's so gifted that at the tender age of twelve, he's the linchpin of the whole organization), so you'd think he would be the one making other people hang back rather than hanging back himself, but the boldly confident Sotoin didn't seem the least bit abashed to have such an eminent figure stand behind him.

As befits a president.

Except that this president isn't even in middle school yet.

As the other members like to say, it's elementary: he's

a fifth grader—Manabu Sotoin, year 5, class A, Yubiwa Academy Elementary School.

In other words, despite being the youngest member of the club, he'd brought this gang of oddballs together—and for some reason, he had the loyalty not only of the child genius but of the perpetually grumpy, rough-mannered delinquent, the proud student council president, and the freewheeling Mr. Bare-Legs as well.

That was the greatest mystery of the Pretty Boy Detective Club, and a point of deep personal interest for me—but at present, I saw no way of unravelling it.

What in the world explained the pull of Manabu the Aesthete…? The truth was, he'd hardly lifted a finger during our last case.

If I had to name one thing he *did* do that time around, it would be dressing as a girl to accompany me when I dressed as a boy (for that matter, what the hell was *I* doing?).

"Well, well, young Dojima! Your eyes are as beautiful as ever! Hyota, your legs look excellent as always. *Nom nom.* And Michiru, you seem to have elevated your cookie-making talents to new heights. I'm counting on you for dinner as well. And you, Nagahiro. Please tell me about the current case in that prideworthy voice. To clarify, I mean your voice, which is worthy of my pride!"

As he arrogantly fired off this litany of compliments and commands, the president plopped down onto the sofa. Some nerve he had, sitting down so self-importantly like that when he'd only just shown up—by comparison, the child genius looked quite modest standing silently behind him.

Although he's always silent.

Silent, cold, and sullen.

That's got to be just about the worst possible character for a genius—in fact, I'd only heard him speak once since we met.

Even when Yubiwa was silent, though, he and Sotoin seemed to enjoy some special mode of communication… And today, they once again appeared to be operating in tandem.

Honestly, what was their connection?

"Yes, Mr. President. As it happens—"

Unlike me, who had met the president only recently, Sakiguchi appeared used to Sotoin's tyrannical behavior, and proceeded to succinctly explain the matter I'd told him about only moments earlier, in that prideworthy (that is, worthy of the president's pride) voice of his.

I couldn't help being surprised at how a simple change in narrator transformed my halting account into an easily comprehensible tale—oddly enough, it was only after hearing his digest of events that I was able to truly digest the bigger picture, even though I myself was the protagonist of the story.

But understanding the big picture didn't help me

understand what it all meant, and I found it somewhat problematic that hearing Nagahiro the Orator recount the story in his beautiful orator's voice almost convinced me that my encounter wasn't so unusual after all, as if the mystery had ceased to be mysterious—could a story be *too* well told?

"Hmm! How interesting! A man who vanishes into thin air, that truly is a mystery!" the leader exclaimed, slapping his knee. Fortunately he seemed resistant to the brainwashing power of the Orator's beautiful voice—and like the other three, he appeared unmoved by the mention of a hundred thousand, or even a million, yen.

I hardly need mention Yubiwa's response.

To a boy who runs an entire foundation, a million yen is probably chump change—and he was indeed gazing at the bills on the table as if they had no value whatsoever. For my part, I looked at that money with a commoner's hungry eye; as they say, he who laughs at one yen will cry over one yen later (I had no intention of laughing at a hundred thousand yen, but I could definitely see myself crying over it).

"Hmm? What's the matter, Sosaku?" Sotoin asked, glancing over his shoulder. "Seems you have something you'd like to say."

I was facing Yubiwa head-on and I couldn't detect any change in his demeanor, so how in the world could Sotoin have picked up on something when he wasn't even *looking* at the child genius? He must just make it up as he goes along.

But in response to his question, Yubiwa raised his eyebrows ever so slightly—a signal subtler even than the blink of an eye.

"Oho, so this is what you're after?" Sotoin asked, plucking a ten-thousand-yen bill from the table and passing it over his shoulder. The child genius took the rectangular piece of paper and began to scrutinize it.

Could it be that he'd never seen such a paltry sum of money before...?

Aside from the leader, the other members appeared as puzzled by Yubiwa's actions as I was: Sakiguchi, the delinquent, and Mr. Bare-Legs all watched and waited for his next move.

But, in something of an anticlimax, the child genius simply handed the bill back to the leader as if he'd grown bored with it.

What? He hadn't discovered anything?

Then why act so suggestively, I wanted to complain (of course, as a student at Yubiwa Academy, I could never complain to the scion of the Yubiwa Foundation about anything, even as a joke).

"I see," Sotoin announced with a dramatic nod, as if he alone had gleaned some satisfaction from Yubiwa's performance.

"What, Mr. President? What is it?"

Apparently, Sakiguchi had reached the limit of his patience with the inscrutable exchange passing between Sotoin and Yubiwa.

"Oh, nothing important," the leader responded, grinning gleefully. "Sosaku was just saying that this bill is counterfeit."

5. A Product of Amusement

Sorry to repeat myself, but Yubiwa—Sosaku Yubiwa—is a child genius. That term could very well refer to the gift for business that allows him to run the Yubiwa Foundation at the age of twelve, but the truth is, his more quintessential talents lie in the realm of art.

Sosaku the Artiste, creator of beauty.

That's his nickname in the club—and in fact, most of the gorgeous works of art on display in the art room are his creations.

That probably explains how he managed to detect something unnatural in the bills lying on the table—an artist's sensitivity, I suppose.

Which I lack. As do most people.

"This is counterfeit…?" Sakiguchi asked in disbelief, picking up another bill. The delinquent and Mr. Bare-Legs followed suit. Actually, Mr. Bare-Legs tried to pick up a bill with his foot, but since this turned out to be more or less impossible, he gave up.

Come on, do you really need to look so disappointed?

In danger of losing the thread of the narrative as I wondered just how much he stakes his life on his legs, I gingerly reached for a bill—a ten-thousand-yen bill—myself.

There was Yukichi Fukuzawa's portrait, and there was the watermark, right where it should be... Looked authentic to me.

But that was the judgement of a layperson.

Banknotes represent the culmination of Japan's technological skill—you could even call their creation a form of art—and I'd heard they're equipped with quite a few security features. The child genius must have found a flaw in one of those. Even the slightest inferiority would tip off the sensitive young artiste—or so I assumed.

"Tsk tsk tsk. Not at all, young Dojima. Sosaku tells me the quality is in fact *too high*."

For some reason, the president wagged his finger smugly.

Man, that pisses me off.

You didn't do anything!

Well, maybe it's like soccer—apparently true connoisseurs of the game admire skilled passers more than the players who actually score the goals... But, what? The quality is too high?

The child genius said that?

I glanced over at him, but his face remained as sullen

41

and unreadable as ever—of all the club members, he was the only one I still wasn't sure had accepted me.

But I wouldn't get anywhere if I let suspicion consume me.

"The quality is too high, you say... Hmm," murmured Sakiguchi, returning the bill to the table as if he'd decided it would be impossible to pass judgement himself. "Are you suggesting that they've ignored any question of cost performance in making these counterfeits? For example, that they've spent more than ten thousand yen to produce a ten-thousand-yen bill?"

"Precisely. Well said. I bestow my praise upon you," Sotoin (the fifth grader) replied arrogantly.

How could a guy with that kind of attitude be so well liked?

"Spending more than ten thousand yen to make a ten-thousand-yen bill... What would be the point of that?"

Unfittingly for a club member, I directed my question not to the leader but to the sub-leader—in this group of eccentrics and oddballs, Sakiguchi at least held the respectable position of student council president in the outside world, so I inevitably found myself trying to draw him out.

Of course, considering his fiancée, I had to admit he might actually outdo them all when it came to shady appetites...

"An excellent question," he answered in his excellent voice. "Naturally, it means that one would be able to produce a bill that appears more genuine than the genuine article."

"More genuine—than the genuine article?"

"Usually, when counterfeit money is detected, a low manufacturing budget is to blame. But if you spend more money than they spend making the real thing, you have a good chance of producing a believable copy of just about anything."

"..."

After hearing Sakiguchi's explanation, I turned my attention once again to the bill in my hand—but there was no way this ten-thousand-yen note was worth more than ten thousand yen.

And even if it were.

Even if they'd gone over-budget on this ten-thousand-yen note—this hundred-thousand-yen broccoli wad—or the million-yen bundle of cash.

If that was what it all meant, then wasn't it pretty meaningless? I felt like I might lose sight of the meaning of meaning.

"Oh, you're kidding me. They made this just to amuse themselves? As a toy?" Mr. Bare-Legs drawled in a bored tone, flapping one of the—counterfeit?—banknotes around in the air.

He really was treating the bill like a toy, but he'd reached that conclusion a little too quickly for my taste. I couldn't be sure, but I didn't think he had it right—

though this sort of thing might well fit the definition of an amusement.

"Bo~ring. Fake or real, it doesn't change the fact that it's still not the kind of thing a real businessman carries around in his pocket."

The delinquent's position was a bit closer to my own than was Mr. Bare-Legs'.

Though if you ask me, a guy carrying around a wad of counterfeit money sounds a hell of a lot more dangerous than a guy carrying around a million yen.

Best to stay away from this character.

In a sense, I'd used the morning's events as a pretext for coming to the art room, but it looked like I might actually have brought in a doozy of a case—and I shivered at the thought.

If I was going to do an about-face, now was the time.

I honestly wanted to side with the delinquent rather than Mr. Bare-Legs, but this was no time to be sharing personal opinions.

Oh geez, it was just play money? I'm sorry guys, I made a fuss over nothing. I'm sure that businessman was just messing with me! Let's drop the whole subject! Fukuroi, would you mind pouring me another cup of tea? I think I'm ready to try your standard Darjeeling blend this time around ♪

Eee ♪

I was hoping to use a little speech like that to change the subject, but since I'm absolutely not the kind of sunny character who ends her sentences with musical notes, all that came out was a stifled, "Buh…"

Tongue-tied by the guy in the tie?

What in the world could the mysterious businessman get out of spending so much money to mess with a regular person like me? I was trying to force the evidence into a narrative that equated counterfeit money with a silly trick, but who plays a trick that would be cheaper to play using real money?

You'd have to be way more serious about the whole thing.

It was precisely this feeling that made me try so hard to turn it into a joke we could all laugh off—which was about the only thing a rookie member who'd accidentally brought a nasty problem to the club *could* do—but being the gloomy type that I am, I just stood there with the words caught in my throat, saying, "Buh… Buh…" over and over again.

"Beautiful!" Sotoin—that is, Manabu the Aesthete—shouted at the top of his lungs.

As if he was finishing my choked-off sentence for me.

Hey, that's not what I was going to say!

But he just kept going.

"Counterfeit money that costs more than its face value to produce—is that not a truly beautiful idea? It sparkles with indescribable brilliance. I can't contain my curiosity!"

6. The Beauty Sensor

Speaking of which, the only thing Sotoin had said about the man's puzzling disappearance into thin air was that it was "interesting"—so if there had been any time to do an about-face, that would've been it.

Since the mood had already taken a pretty unsettling turn by that point, I probably could've managed it—but now it was too late.

My warning sensor was too dull, and Sotoin's beauty sensor had gone off first. I suppose any act that ignores cost performance—which is to say, that goes beyond profit and loss or personal interest—fits his aesthetic to a tee.

And once things reached that point, there was no stopping him.

Although I have to admit one thing.

The sort of refined, or perhaps...elegant spirit of play that ignores the bottom line strikes me as an essential element of artistic creation. I can't deny that I, too, thought the act of creating over-budget counterfeit money was in and of itself beautiful.

But everything depends on context.

I hardly need to point this out, but producing counterfeit money is a crime. The crime of improper currency forgery or something like that—and I'm fairly sure it's quite a serious charge.

If I accepted Sakiguchi's analysis of the situation, then this was no time to be worrying about Mr. Bare-Legs' aversion to the police—we had to get serious about handing that hundred thousand yen in (fake) bills over to the cops.

But as far as I could tell from Sotoin's beaming face, he had no intention whatsoever of taking that course of action—no question about it, he planned to solve this mystery himself.

Which meant it was virtually meaningless to resist— from the student council president and the delinquent to Mr. Bare-Legs and, of course, the child genius stationed behind Sotoin like a bodyguard, all were loyal to der leader in der own special ways.

Come to think of it, this regime was outrageously autocratic.

Even if we put it to a democratic vote, I'd lose by a five-to-one landslide—which meant arguing for my position as the minority wouldn't just be meaningless, it would be downright counterproductive.

In which case, a more productive approach would be to weasel my way into the regime by pretending to agree with the dictator, from which position I could subtly urge caution, hint at danger, and steer us all away from the jaws of death.

Crap.

How did I, the girl who had completely ignored relationship-building skills for practically a decade, suddenly get caught up in all this politicking? But, no exaggeration, if I didn't start directing the show from the shadows, the Pretty Boy Detective Club could be headed for total annihilation.

"What's with that face, Dojima? You look like one of those hot-blooded young people who actually believes politicians when they say, 'We need your precious vote!' What we actually need is grassroots mobilization on a massive scale."

Awfully satirical for someone who doesn't even know what I'm thinking.

Plus, my precious vote *does* matter!

Do you even realize how much responsibility is getting put on me here? Mostly by myself, but still.

Why did I even come to these guys for help in the first place….

I can only conclude that I wasn't merely deluded, I was delusional.

"Come on, Dojima. I'll accept that a guy like me can't

tell play money from the real thing, but you're telling me that even with your crazy eyesight, you couldn't see through a little trick like this?"

"Ouch…"

That one stung.

If I'd realized the money was counterfeit when I picked up the bundle of bills Mr. Businessman (who I was now certain was not in fact a businessman) had dropped, I probably could have settled the matter on my own.

If I'd realized the seriousness of the situation, I probably would have pretended not to notice the money lying there on the ground in the first place—which was a thought that made me wretchedly regretful.

"You have a point there, Michiru. It's quite unlike Mayumi the Seer, she of the beautiful eyes, to overlook something like that."

Sotoin cocked his head innocently.

Hey, don't give people nicknames without their permission!

Mayumi the Seer? What the hell!

"It's not like my eyes make me clairvoyant or something," I pouted, mentally cursing him (although secretly I wasn't at all unhappy that the leader seemed to have accepted me as a member). "Plus," I added, "I was wearing my glasses, so what do you expect?"

"Your glasses, young Dojima? Ah yes, that's right. The ones you use to restrict your greatest beauty—your vision."

He sounded satisfied with my excuse.

The president always used to harangue me about taking off my glasses so he could see my "beautiful eyes," but ever since he learned that I wear them to protect my overly good eyesight from overuse, he'd actually stopped doing that.

I suppose when it came down to it, even Manabu the Aesthete—who not only valued beauty above all else but was willing to ignore all else for the sake of beauty—had to draw the line somewhere if he was going to hold onto his humanity. Or perhaps the placement of that line itself was a part of his aesthetic. Though it didn't make a lick of sense to me.

Still, the fact of the matter was that I didn't have to be quite so uptight about protecting my eyes—overusing them would be bad, but using them here and there was fine. Sometimes I even forgot to wear my glasses, so essentially it was no different from wearing contact lenses for me.

And so, while I couldn't undo my mistake, I could take a closer look at the banknotes—I placed one hand on either side of the frames and carefully removed my glasses (I do have a spare pair, but they're expensive, so naturally I tend to handle them carefully).

Now let's see here.

If I used my real vision—the vision that allows me

to find stars that don't exist, the vision that even I have to admit is frankly somewhat unbelievable—would I be able to determine the authenticity of this bill?

Sizzle.

"Huh?"

7. The Money Envelope

Sizzle…

Sizzle sizzle sizzle…

I gazed intently at the bill, a scorching noise playing in my mind as I used my true vision at full bore, but I still couldn't distinguish it from the real thing—yeah right.

Telling them apart was a cinch.

I might not have the child genius's artistic eye for beauty, the eye of an appraiser, but when it came to plain old eyesight, I had him beat—and this was certainly no Bank-of-Japan-issued banknote.

The solution to this game of Spot the Mistake was literally obvious at a glance—there were quite a few small differences. I was forced to agree that the quality was "too high," as the child genius had said (or rather, as Sotoin had said he'd said).

I felt more like I was looking at a precision machine than a piece of art—interesting. So this was what could be achieved when money was no object in the production of counterfeit money.

But I didn't blurt out "Huh?" because I was transfixed by the outstanding workmanship—in that case, I probably would have come out with something more like "Wow!"

Apparently I didn't just lack an eye for artistic beauty, I lacked any and all receptivity to beautiful things—after all, even my stomach hadn't been able to handle Michiru the Epicure's culinary creations until I got used to them.

So the reason my "Huh" had a question mark after it rather than an exclamation point was that it wasn't the bill's quality which had caught my attention—my eyes had been drawn to the *inside*. That's right, the inside.

Of the bill.

A back side, sure, but does a bill even have an inside?

Unable to believe my own eyes, I flipped the bill over in my hand, but I still saw the same thing.

From the front and from the back.

What I saw was a piece of paper inside the bill—but it was only when I triple-checked from the side that I was certain.

Something was definitely "sandwiched" in there.

Inside that bill measuring a mere tenth of a millimeter thick.

"What's wrong, Doji? You look like a real miser staring at the money like that. Whatever's bugging you,

I suggest you calm yourself with a nice, soothing look at my legs."

Caught off guard by Mr. Bare-Legs' comment, I couldn't help taking advantage of his kindness—but what would I do if his legs really did calm me down?

Anyway.

"Well, it's just, there seems to be something inside this bill."

"Inside the bill? What the hell are you talking about, kid?"

The delinquent seemed confused—which was an entirely reasonable reaction. I didn't even feel confident about the statement myself.

To the contrary, there probably wasn't a person in the world who trusted my eyes less than I did.

They'd given me the runaround for ten whole years.

So I checked the remaining nine bills—and came up with the same result each time.

All hundred thousand yen's worth of banknotes had something inside.

Each bill was constructed like an ultra-thin envelope—which in a way must have taken even greater skill than the counterfeiting itself. What kind of super-fine tweezers must they have used to make something like that?

"No shit? Well then…"

The delinquent still looked suspicious, but he picked

up one of the bills and went to tear it down the middle—I guess he was so curious about this something even someone who could see through things couldn't fully identify that he was willing to resort to brute force to solve the mystery, but just at that moment, someone grabbed his arm.

It was the child genius.

He shook his head silently.

Maybe, as an artist, he was informing his senior club member that whether the object in question was counterfeit or illegal, valuable or valueless, handling it so violently was unacceptable—which to me was an incomprehensible standard of behavior, but the delinquent did give up his attempt to tear the bill in half, and instead asked awkwardly, "What's your deal, Sosaku? What do *you* suggest we do?"

"Ahem. Michiru," Sotoin began, stepping in as interpreter. "Sosaku is saying, 'Leave it to *this guy*.'"

The leader was always butting into other people's business and saying whatever he felt like—but wait, Sosaku refers to himself as "this guy"?

That didn't exactly fit my image.

"Well, if he says so…" the delinquent responded, handing the bill that had so narrowly escaped destruction over to the child genius—who proceeded to do essentially the same thing the delinquent had just tried to do.

While Michiru the Epicure had tried to tear the bill down the middle, Sosaku the Artiste tried to tear the front and back apart—and not just tried, but actually did.

With the utmost care.

Just like he was peeling a sticker off its backing.

The child genius succeeded in separating an already paper-thin bill into two halves—and with his bare hands at that, no tweezers or knife or anything. He did it with such extraordinary skill that I almost wondered if all bills were made of two layers to begin with, like the outer and inner shells of a winter coat.

The resident artiste of the Pretty Boy Detective Club was indeed living up to his reputation… But this was no time to lose myself in admiration for his craftsmanship.

What demanded attention.

What demanded *my* attention was the slip of paper that had fluttered to the carpet when the child genius so adroitly pulled the bill apart.

The paper was nearly as big as the bill itself, but folded in half—and as far as I could tell, it was made of the same sort of paper as the bill.

"What have we here."

Sotoin bent over and plucked it off the ground.

Apparently, the boy who knows only beauty knows no fear.

He proceeded to fearlessly unfold the bill—his movements flowing so smoothly that I'm quite sure he would have done the same thing, with the same "what have we here," even if the object that had fallen out of the bill was the detonator for a bomb.

"Oho! Looky here, lads. I believe I am holding in my hands an invitation."

An invitation?

8. The Invitation

Congratulations!

You have in your hands one ticket to the Reasonable Doubt Casino.

Doors open every Sunday night. Please come to the address below in casual dress. Do not bring guests and tell no one of your plans.

Location:

Gymnasium #2, Kamikazari Middle School

9. Sunday Plans

"Looks like a scam!"

The first words out of my mouth gave away my unvarnished thoughts on the matter.

My nefarious scheme had been to lurk in the shadows and slyly manipulate the Pretty Boy Detective Club, but at this rate that kind of Trojan Horse-type plan was looking less and less tenable.

Although it wasn't like I intended to oppose every decision the leader made.

Honestly, though, "Congratulations"?!

"Tell no one of your plans"?!

Every single line was suspicious!

Thankfully, the delinquent reinforced my frank assessment by noting cynically, "The way it's written *is* pretty fishy—it's an invitation, sure, but I feel like it's welcoming us to the highway to hell."

On top of that, the invitation had come inside a counterfeit bill—which if you ask me adds up to a double helping of dubious, with an extra side of suspicious.

In any case, the fact that an invitation was sandwiched inside this bill left no room for doubt that the hundred thousand yen (and the million yen) were counterfeit—and no sooner had that thought crossed my mind than the child genius set about pulling apart the other bills, one after another.

His hands moved so dexterously that you could be forgiven for thinking this was his day job—although in truth, this first-year middle school student's real job wasn't even studying, it was running a foundation.

Of course, invitations fluttered down from inside the other bills as well (even if there didn't seem to be space enough inside them)—as if we were watching a magic trick.

I was curious to see if he would tear them all open, but he stopped at the sixth one, and, with the six invitations lined up on the table, returned to his post behind Sotoin.

Six invitations…

Since they all said, "Do not bring guests and tell no one of your plans," each must be valid for only one person, which must mean six invitations were enough for six people, right?

Wait a minute, six people?

That just happened to be the same number of people in the art room!

Wonder why he stopped there...

"So they're open every Sunday, are they? Lads, I take it you're all free this coming Sunday?"

"I'm free."

"Free as a bird."

"My schedule is clear."

For real?

Leaving aside the delinquent, Mr. Bare-Legs was an ace member of the track team and Sakiguchi was president of the student council. I highly doubted they could free up their schedules that easily.

It was weird that a group of boys their age could even hang out like this after school in the first place—when I thought about it like that, I realized that even without getting involved in this case, the club itself was like a candle in the wind.

Maybe I didn't need to worry so much about having brought them a nasty case—the club was bound for extinction before long anyway, regardless of what I did to help or harm.

Still, I didn't think I'd be able to sleep very well if the group went under because of me.

"And what about you, young Dojima? You didn't answer. Do you have plans?"

"Um... Let me think...."

I pulled out my lily-white, unsullied student planner and pretended to check my schedule. What kind of cheap trick was I playing? Now that I'd quit sneaking up to the roof after school to stargaze, I never had any plans to speak of.

After making this pretentious show, I could very well have lied to them—for instance, if I said I always went to the mountains to escape the heat on the weekends (never mind that it was almost winter), that would have gotten me out of going to the casino with them.

But if I did that, I wouldn't have been able to achieve my supreme goal of keeping an eye on them—which meant it was time to humbly and honestly admit that my calendar was completely empty.

"Hmm, it looks as if I can manage to free up some time. My schedule is full for the next three years straight, but I believe I can make an exception and clear my plans this Sunday night."

It was impossible.

My brain utterly rejected humility and honesty.

On top of that, I was lousy at lying—what middle school student has plans all the way through graduation?

What do I do if pretentiousness turns out to be my only strong suit?

"You can? I'm delighted to hear that." The smiling So-toin accepted my lie without a fuss—perhaps this generosity of spirit was the secret to his mysterious popularity. "Excellent! Well then, it's settled. Let's all meet on Sunday night and proceed together to the address below—um, how do you read these characters?"

The leader couldn't read the name of the venue.

Perhaps that was inevitable since he was only in fifth grade—but, he was planning to accept the invitation without even being able to read it?

He was way too reckless.

"It says, 'Gymnasium #2, Kamikazari Middle School,' Mr. President," the vice president said, coming to his aid.

"Kamikazari Middle School? Why, I believe I've heard that name before. Hmm, must've been involved in some past case. Heh, I sense a vague connection," Sotoin muttered, seemingly lost in thought.

If all you did was look at his face, you might mistake him for a famous detective chasing down the solution to a case, but in reality the familiarity of the name had nothing to do with a past case.

Kamikazari is a middle school near Yubiwa Academy—the connection wasn't vague, it was concrete as could be.

In fact, it's so close by you can see it from the roof of our own school (with my eyesight, anyway).

…But being neighbors didn't mean we were friends—to the contrary, the two schools traditionally clashed.

Kamikazari was our rival.

Come to think of it, Sotoin and I nearly had a nasty run-in with some Kamikazari students the other day in the course of our detective work—but the president appeared to have forgotten all about that.

I guess he only remembers beautiful things.

Setting aside the question of the leader's brain (and setting aside the question of whether something so important should be set aside), the school name written on the invitation didn't strike me as overwhelmingly unnatural.

A minute earlier I'd gotten carried away and thought to myself that every single line of it was suspicious, but actually, the one reading "Gymnasium #2, Kamikazari Middle School" gave the whole invitation a certain plausibility.

Which is to say, I'd heard about this.

I'd heard rumors to the effect that there was gambling at the school on a nightly basis, and that girls should never under any circumstances go anywhere near it because it was extremely dangerous—which was unsettling, even if the "on a nightly basis" part was an embellishment.

The rumor was as seemingly unreliable as the one about a Pretty Boy Detective Club operating at our own school, but considering that the Pretty Boy Detective Club actually existed, it wouldn't be that strange if the casino existed as well.

Even so, what was I supposed to make of the proviso about girls never under any circumstances going anywhere near it…?

"What are you worried about? Right now, you're not a girl, you're a pretty boy," the delinquent spat out coldly, before adding, "Anyway, you'll be with us, so I doubt anything crazy will happen."

Apparently, he was incapable of being considerate without pretending to be nasty first.

"Yeah! We'll be there with you, so you don't need to worry about a thing, Doji," Mr. Bare-Legs added blithely.

Come to think of it, he was the one who should be fearing for his safety, not me—a guy who gets kidnapped at a rate of once every four years ought to think twice before going into dangerous parts of town.

"In any case," the councilman pronounced, "it may be counterfeit, and more than half of it may be ripped to pieces, but we really must go so you can return the money to your Mr. Businessman."

Right, that's what this was all about to begin with— we weren't going on an undercover mission to investigate overly-high-quality counterfeit money, we were following through on my request to find a missing person.

I think the reason Sakiguchi looked so gloomy must've been that, in his capacity as student council president, he of course knew more about those disturbing rumors than I did, and therefore had a better sense of the very real threats we might face in our visit to Kamikazari Middle.

Or maybe, despite the fact that he'd announced his

availability so quickly, he actually had a date with his fiancée scheduled for Sunday night—in which case, you could say we had just saved an innocent girl from the clutches of a pervert.

I felt like I'd just accomplished something positive, even though I hadn't done a thing.

"Considering the relationship between Yubiwa Academy and Kamikazari Middle, we certainly can't go in our uniforms—though it does say to come in 'casual dress.'"

"What does casual dress mean again? Like, ordinary clothes? The only ordinary clothes I own are shorts…" said the boy whose school uniform also consists of shorts, displaying no common sense whatsoever. He probably didn't even want to wear shoes—but the problem wasn't the definition of shorts, it was the definition of casual dress.

Of course, casual dress means ordinary clothes, like what you'd wear around the house, but if we genuinely showed up looking like slobs, we'd be dying of embarrassment.

"It's what some call somewhat formal dress," I explained.

"I see, somewhat formal," Sotoin responded with a nod.

A somewhat worrisome nod.

10. Somewhat Formal Dress

And so, before I knew what was happening, we'd decided to visit the gym of a certain middle school on Sunday night—but before we set out, I was going to need a little work.

As I've already mentioned a number of times, I—that is, Mayumi Dojima, Yubiwa Academy, year 2, class B—dress as a boy on a daily basis, but since I do the dressing up myself, I can't say the level of accuracy is very high.

I might look like a male student from a distance, but despite the slacks and the short hair, if you took a good look at me from close up you'd know I was a girl.

At the very least, it would be easier to tell that Mayumi Dojima is a girl than it would to tell that she's a twisted, obstinate, gloomy grouch.

Therefore, when it came to marching into a danger zone as a member of the Pretty Boy Detective Club (the obvious danger of marching into Kamikazari Middle School as students of Yubiwa Academy aside, doing anything with the Pretty Boy Detective Club seemed plenty risky on its own), I needed to up the level of my drag game a little—er, a lot.

I had to get fixed up so no one would figure out I was actually a girl—and that meant the time had come for our resident costume artist to do his thing.

Sosaku the Artiste.

I needed to ask a favor of the child genius who maybe, or rather quite likely, still didn't accept me as a member of the club—after all, he was the one who had managed to turn me into a boy for the first time in my life the other day.

Setting aside personal feelings, he at least seemed to accept me as raw material for his art, so on Sunday I arrived early at the art room and he helped me morph into a magnificent boy yet again.

His skill with makeup was astonishing and his touch with the barber's shears worthy of amazement—wait, we're not using a wig this time? We're actually going to cut my hair? But, I already cut it pretty short myself, didn't I?

After that, he gave me a set of "casual dress" clothes that he'd altered to fit me, or more likely, sewn from scratch—which more or less fit the image of "casual dress" I'd had in mind.

For a scion of the Yubiwa Foundation, they may have been more like loungewear, but for a commoner like me, they were nothing if not dress-up clothes.

Naturally, Yubiwa himself, as well as the other members of the club who trickled into the art room after us, were all wearing what I'd call party clothes rather than casual attire (most likely haute couture numbers pulled together by their exclusive stylist). Even Mr. Bare-Legs' shorts looked more like something off the Paris runways than a casual item of clothing.

Together they amounted to such a technicolor rainbow that I felt like I'd go blind even with my glasses on—if this was "somewhat casual," then I couldn't wait to see their version of "informal" someday.

"Oho, young Dojima, you've been done up! And thanks to you, Sosaku looks quite pleased with himself. Hahaha, what a beautiful exchange between fellow members!"

The perpetually high-spirited Sotoin seemed to be in especially high spirits tonight—although only the gods knew if Yubiwa was actually feeling pleased with himself.

"Well lads, shall we? The Pretty Boy Detective Club is on the case! As always, let us be beautiful, let us be boys, and let us be detectives!"

"Sure," "Yup," "Yes, let's," answered the delinquent, Mr. Bare-Legs, and the councilman in turn—with the child genius following silently after them.

Every time I witnessed their harmonious teamwork, I couldn't help feeling inferior, like there was no room for me to join in—but thanks to the artiste, I was a pretty boy for the moment, even if only on the surface.

Mayumi the Seer, she (he?) of the beautiful eyes.

So.

"And let us be a team," I mumbled, as I accompanied them out the door.

11. Territory

"As long as people talk about 'exclusive economic zones,' true friendship between nations'll never exist."

So said not some great man, but our school's resident satirist—though considering that even middle school students have territories they forbid one another to enter, what can you really say about it?

But that night, the Pretty Boy Detective Club (myself included) barged calmly across the line separating the territory of the private Yubiwa Academy from that of the private Kamikazari Middle School.

Even disguised as a boy, my heart was pounding.

I felt like I was doing something much worse than sneaking onto the school roof in the middle of the night— not to mention that I was about to enter a middle school I didn't even attend.

"H-Have you all been here before? I mean, inside Kamikazari Middle…"

Their bold attitude made me think one of their past

cases must have involved such a thing, but I was wrong.

"Oh no, never," replied Sakiguchi. "We've had some interactions with them in the past, it's true, but this is our first time visiting the premises."

Which meant that while these pretty boys may not have been curvaceous, they were certainly courageous— for my part, I was terrified about what might wait in store for us.

"Have no fear. I am still the president of the student council—and if I say I'm here to look into reports of unrest occurring near our school, they'll believe me."

The vice president used his trusted and powerful position in the official world with surprising savvy—although in terms of "unrest," the Pretty Boy Detective Club caused plenty of it themselves.

"Hahaha. Relax, young Dojima. No one will give us any trouble. Unless being beautiful is a crime, that is!" The excited president completely ignored the vice president's words.

I don't know about beauty being a crime, but one reason he didn't feel especially guilty sneaking into another middle school was probably that he traipsed around ours all the time like he owned the place, even though he was only in fifth grade.

"You seem to be having fun, too, Sosaku. Excellent. At this rate, we may just be lucky enough to witness one of your patented soft-shoe routines tonight!"

As far as I could tell, the child genius looked the same as always, but anyway...

A soft-shoe routine?

The child genius? Dancing??

Or was the president talking about Sosaku making him a pair of slippers?

"You're talking about sneaking in, Dojima, but the gates are wide open. And I didn't see a single car in the lot, so the dear teachers must've all gone home. You ask me, this feels like a warm welcome," the delinquent announced, though I'm not sure if his confidence came from being a member of a detective organization or being part of the criminal underworld. Apparently, he'd been casually keeping an eye on our surroundings on the way in.

Well, we *had* been invited.

If the gate had been closed, that would have been the end of it—which would've been great, but then this book would never have been written. So we walked onto the grounds of that middle school that wasn't ours, followed the map printed on the invitations, and arrived at Gymnasium #2.

According to some fairly plausible rumors circulating among the girls at our school, the inside of Kamikazari Middle should've resembled a drawing of hell, but actually, the row of buildings, the tidy flower beds, and even Gymnasium #2 were very clean and neat—rumors can be so unreliable.

As for the veracity of the rumors about the Pretty Boy Detective Club—well, for the present, I'll withhold judgement.

"Looks like they've got curtains up so we can't see what's going on inside—guess our only choice is to head on in."

Mr. Bare-Legs—who was bare-legged even in the middle of a near-winter night—actually sounded excited.

The boy with the beautiful legs liked to gambol, so maybe he liked to gamble, too.

Of course, if I felt like it (and took off my glasses) I could have looked through not just the heavy curtains but the walls themselves to see what was happening inside the gym, but there was no point in spoiling their fun.

We walked around to the front of the gym, reached for the steel doors that were shut as tight as the curtains—and.

12. The Reasonable Doubt Casino

Even if something as fanciful as a nighttime casino inside a school gym really did exist, my powers of imagination—which are much feebler than my powers of sight—had utterly failed to come up with an image of what it might look like until that moment.

If pressed, I might have envisioned something along the lines of a school festival—a heartwarmingly ramshackle scene.

But the panorama spread out before my eyes was completely different from that idyllic vision. Inside Gymnasium #2 was a terrifyingly real casino.

Poker tables, slot machines, roulette wheels, all lined up at even intervals around the room like in a movie. The dealers cutting cards looked completely authentic in both dress and manner, and there were even girls in bunny outfits carrying around trays of drinks. I was stunned.

There were quite a few guests, as well.

From a quick scan of the room, I estimated around

fifty people gambling and maybe ten dealers, which made for a surprisingly lively, even boisterous atmosphere.

The lights were turned up as bright as they would go, and instrumental music was blasting at top volume—for a casino operating at night in a school gym, there was nothing stealthy about this.

It was like an alternate universe.

I felt like the entrance to the gym was an Anywhere Door that led straight to a hotel in Las Vegas—although the generally young age of the guests and staff (bunny girls included) was one clue to the contrary.

Oh, everyone was dressed to the nines, no question about that.

Still, they had to be in their teens—no.

To be honest, the boys and girls alike looked like middle school students.

Based on that point alone, the scene did slightly resemble a school festival—but just how much money had gone into creating this casino? I couldn't even begin to guess.

This place gave the alternate universe I'd encountered the first time I opened the art room door a run for its money. Actually, in terms of scale alone, the fact that they'd commandeered the gym like this and completely transformed it into a casino might very well have the art room beat.

"Welcome," a bunny girl greeted us as I stood there

dumbfounded.

Even as a girl, I would have done a double take at her outfit.

But right now, I was a boy.

How was a pretty boy supposed to act in a situation like this? I glanced at the five guys standing next to me, but none of them were looking at the bunny girl—they all seemed to have zeroed in on the games behind her.

What were they, children?

No—boys?

Mr. Bare-Legs might later regret not having seen the bunny girl, but for the sake of protecting her fishnet stockings, I knew I had to do the listening for all six of us.

I would take care of the tutorial, since they all seemed like the type to skip the instruction manual and just start playing anyway.

"Apologies for the inconvenience, but would you mind showing me your invitations?"

"Oh, of course… Here they are."

I handed her the six invitations, wondering as I did so if she might actually be younger than me, even though her makeup and bunny ears made her look grown-up (weird logic, I know).

"Excellent. Thank you very much," she said with a smile. "You can get your chips at the purchase booth on the righthand side of the stage—and you'll want to cash them in at the cashier's booth on the left."

The cashier's booth.

I sucked in my cheeks at the word.

Right.

The guests and staff were all so young—children, even—that I'd been thinking of the casino as akin to a school fair or a children's game despite its seeming authenticity, but I was wrong.

Boy was I wrong.

A casino where this level of gambling took place was no childish game—real money was at play here.

Not counterfeit money.

Wait, even the counterfeit money had taken a lot of real money to make—and that invitation was way too over the top to be the product of a playful spirit.

"Beverages are complimentary, so please order whatever you'd like. And if you have any further questions, please don't hesitate to ask. Oh, and one more thing," the bunny girl said, holding out several masks.

They weren't the kind of masks you wear to keep from catching a cold; instead of covering your mouth, they were meant to hide the upper half of your face—like the masks rich people wear at fancy balls.

Or put more simply, the kind of masks Tuxedo Mask wears.

"Photography and video recording are prohibited here, but if you have further concerns about privacy, we would be happy to lend you these masks. Would you like to use them?"

"I'm not sure…"

Now that she mentioned it, I saw that quite a few of the guests were wearing similar masks—I hadn't noticed before because they blended in so well with the fancy dress, but now the level of anonymity struck me as strange.

"What do you want to do, guys?" I asked my fellow club members.

"What? M-Masks? To hide our f-faces? …Wh-Whatever for?"

For once, Sotoin appeared shaken—apparently, he was struggling to understand what possible purpose there could be in the foolish act of hiding one's beautiful face.

The idea of anonymity never even occurred to him.

"Well, if that's our leader's decision," Sakiguchi sighed, shrugging his shoulders.

His face was better known than the rest of ours because of his official post, so he might actually have had more reason to desire anonymity, but all the same he seemed intent on helping the leader save face—literally.

I suppose clandestine activity is basically impossible for the members of the Pretty Boy Detective Club anyway—no mask could hide their flamboyant brilliance.

To be completely honest, I wasn't personally opposed to wearing one, since I have a typical teenager's fear of getting in trouble with her parents, but I couldn't buck the consensus—and anyway, who cares? I'd already given up my dreams for the future.

"We don't need them. We have nothing to hide," I told the bunny girl.

"Very well," she replied, seeming to take genuine pride in her job. "Please enjoy your time here at the Reasonable Doubt Casino!"

13. Let the Games Begin

Enjoy—ha!

She could say what she wanted, but I was a gloomy girl whose sole nighttime activity up till now had been stargazing—and I didn't have the faintest idea how I should act now that I'd been tossed into a casino.

The boys, however, were another story.

"Well, no point in standing around watching. I say we play some games and collect intel from the people around the tables. Everyone good with that?"

"Right. Play some games, that sounds good."

"Please make sure you actually gather some information, Hyota. Don't forget our real mission here."

"Hahaha! Let your wagers showcase the beauty of your aesthetic, lads! We revel in beauty that we may revel beautifully! The games are afoot!"

With that, they split up and swung into action—although the child genius was already in line at the purchase booth.

He hadn't broken into an impromptu celebratory dance number, but I suspect that as an artist, he may have been even more interested in the organization that produced those counterfeit bills than the rest of us.

The chips started at one hundred yen.

That may sound like small change in this era when a hundred yen can hardly buy a can of soda, but it was a pretty hefty minimum bet.

If you think of a hundred yen as roughly one dollar, that comes to around the same price as the cheapest chips in Las Vegas—in other words, the rates were as authentic as the setting, which was enough to sweep away any lingering sense that I was attending an event in a middle school gym.

The same was obvious from observing the skill of the dealers—not a dropped card or poorly tossed roulette ball was to be seen.

Not that I know anything about professional card dealers, but these people definitely seemed like pros— and like the bunny girl who had welcomed us at the door, all the staff appeared to be both good at their jobs and very enthusiastic. Whoever was running this place had clearly poured money into more than just the hardware.

It truly was true to life.

Anyhow, the maskless pretty boys headed off to exchange a thousand yen each, for starters—which gave them each ten chips.

"Uh…"

I guess they could write it off as an operating expense, but seeing real money in play gave me pause.

I'd picked up that counterfeit money Mr. Businessman had dropped, and now five thousand yen was circulating in the world.

If this was a scam, it was an insanely elaborate one, and the scammers clearly didn't care about the cost-performance ratio. But nevertheless, we'd just lost five thousand yen—that is, five thousand yen that we might or might not win back had just vanished into thin air.

I felt vaguely like I'd fallen for a hustle, but I wasn't at all sure the hustler was profiting off this—or if there even was a "hustler."

Since we had no choice but to investigate this place if we wanted to find out, though, I suppose my fellow members were acting appropriately—and I figured I'd better follow suit by getting my own thousand yen's worth of chips. But…

"No, young Dojima," the leader notified me. "Tonight, you'll be observing."

Huh? Observing?

Was he honestly going to give me a moralistic lecture about gambling while I was still in middle school? Wasn't that the pot calling the kettle black?

"Oh no, I very much want you to enjoy yourself. But being Mayumi the Seer, I'm afraid that whatever game you might play, your eyesight would amount to a violation of the rules. Considering you can see right through the spin of the slot machines and roulette wheels, the roll of the dice, even the backs of cards, betting money at a casino is going to be a bit problematic."

"Oh…"

He was so right that I didn't have anything to say.

Playing for fun would be bad enough, but playing for money was clearly out of the question—an excuse like "I can't use my superhuman vision with my glasses on" probably wouldn't hold much water beyond my own circle of friends.

Guess this elementary school Kogoro Akechi does occasionally say sensible things, as if they just popped into his head.

But then, why even bring me?

I'd rather be holding down the fort.

Well, I suppose I did come along voluntarily so I could keep an eye on the activities of the Pretty Boy Detective Club, so it didn't make much sense to complain. And I'd gotten swept up by the atmosphere and accidentally shown a little enthusiasm, but once I cleared my head, I remembered that I don't even like this sort of game in the first place.

I don't play games on my smartphone (I don't even have a smartphone), but that doesn't mean I have some special fondness for low-tech games. The truth is, I didn't even know the rules to most—which is to say basically any—of the games lined up in that casino.

So maybe observer was the perfect role for me.

As guardian of the Pretty Boy Detective Club (ah, what an illustrious title), I must devote myself to watching over them. I tucked the thousand-yen bill back into my wallet.

At least I'd avoided wasting money.

Also, I was curious to see what sort of elegant behavior the five pretty boys would display in this kind of place— each had his own special skill, from aesthetic judgement and oration to beautiful legs, gourmet cooking, and artistic talent, but whether any of those skills were useful for gambling was an open question—ultimately, they were supposed to be collecting information, but how would they join in the fun here?

I realized I'd probably stick out if I just stood there not at least pretending to enjoy myself, so I started strolling around the hall—with a (wine) glass of orange juice I'd gotten from a bunny girl in hand.

"Oh geez!" I blurted out.

While I was wandering around enjoying for just a moment the feeling of being at a resort, our leader had sat down at a blackjack table—blackjack of all things!

He liked the tough stuff, apparently.

I'm not one to talk, but did he even know the rules?

Sometimes I almost forget because of his grandiose

attitude, but the leader is still very much a fifth grader, so when he sits in a chair like that his feet aren't anywhere near the ground. He looked a little ridiculous, but at the same time he didn't seem out of place.

His behavior was very grown-up, or rather, gentlemanly.

He seemed to be not so much playing the game as relishing it.

In that sense, blackjack did seem to suit him—though to me, Black Jack would always be the name of a doctor.

At the next table over, Vice President Sakiguchi was playing poker.

Poker I do know a little bit about. That is, I know some of the hands, but not all the rules... And I'd heard the Japanese rules were different from the rules everywhere else anyway.

The notion that the rules we know basically only amount to house rules was vaguely depressing, but that aside, it seemed like a fitting game for Sakiguchi.

Whatever rules they were playing by, the literal poker face of the student council president, who had used his eloquent bluffing skills to combat a criminal organization during our last case, was definitely suited to poker—plus, an erudite fellow like him probably knew all the international rules anyway.

The person I was really worried about was Mr. Bare-Legs, who seemed liable to get so caught up in enjoying himself that he'd forget all about the mission… And there he was, glued to the roulette wheel.

Roulette just might be the simplest game to understand at a casino—all you have to do is place your bets. Even I could handle that. Still, there must be some trick or method to it, and I suspected Mr. Bare-Legs had even less of a grasp of the game than I did; honestly, it looked like he was just throwing his chips down pretty much at random.

I guess that's one way to play, and it's kind of cute, even—but just as I was feeling charmed by young Hyota's artless innocence, I looked a little closer and realized his actions weren't so cute after all.

He wasn't placing bets randomly, he was betting against the crowd—every single time, he placed his chips on the opposite of the color or numbers the other players chose.

Oh man…

I'd hate it if someone did that to me…

Apparently he wasn't so much betting to win as amusing himself by sowing chaos around the wheel and upsetting the other players—yes, that angelic face of his just might be hiding the most devilish personality of all the Pretty Boys.

But one thing that watching him—and Sotoin and Sakiguchi as well—made abundantly clear was that casinos aren't just about the interaction between dealer and player, or house and guest, if you will—the other strangers at the table are also an indispensable element of the game.

The air was thick with the desire to win big in front of everyone, or to bet more than anyone else—to me, everyone seemed at least as concerned with how other people saw them as they were with winning.

They were *playing*.

I suppose not that many people genuinely dream of winning big at gambling—which meant Mr. Bare-Legs' style of play wouldn't be so unusual, if only he didn't take it so far.

As for the ill-tempered delinquent, I was certain he must be having a ball in this sort of venue, but when I finally spotted him, he was backing away from the baccarat table.

Baccarat… Um, what kind of game was that again?

Blackjack and poker were bad enough, but baccarat? All that name meant to me was a fancy brand of crystal.

Did it have something to do with betting on whether the number would be big or small?

The game seemed to have just ended, so I started walking toward Fukuroi to ask about it, but then made an abrupt U-turn.

His expression was brutally fierce.

Michiru Fukuroi was striding toward the purchase booth looking every inch the bossman, his mouth a tight line and an obvious chip on his shoulder about what I could only guess was a recent loss of chips.

He looked like a wild beast.

" … "

Even though he'd been playing for less than ten minutes, he already seemed to have run through his thousand yen—which meant he'd suffered the picture-perfect loss of a hundred yen per minute.

From behind, he was somehow both totally unapproachable and the veritable embodiment of defeat—and he looked ready to spend the rest of his cash on more chips so he could wreak his revenge.

From my perspective, his indomitable spirit was admirable, but from the casino's, he probably just looked like an easy mark.

As a friend, I wanted to warn him to quit, to say that if he knew the rules of baccarat then he should also learn the one about cutting one's losses, but sorry, I was way too scared.

To tell the truth, just the sight of him walking away like that was enough to make me want to give up on being his friend entirely.

Actually, we might be members of the same club, but we weren't really friends yet—and with that thought in mind, I hurried away from the dangerous individual.

Plotting unscrupulously to gain the upper hand in our relationship by comforting him once he'd run through all his money and ended up penniless, I looked around for the last member of the club: the child genius. That guy's good at disappearing, and once you lose sight of him, it can be tough to find him again.

Just when I'd started to consider taking off my glasses to search for him, I spotted him sitting in front of a slot machine—slots, huh?

Unlike the table games, with slots you don't have to compete with a dealer, let alone interact with the other guests.

It's a completely solitary pursuit, the machine itself your only opponent.

Kind of like a video game—except that these days, even video games connect you to other players online.

What can I say?

Basically, this kid likes to be by himself, I guess—he's the acting director of a massive foundation for crying out loud, but no matter how bursting with talent he might be, the role is definitely a bad fit on a personal level.

Throwing pottery, drawing pictures, hell, turning gloomy girls into pretty boys—those are much more to his liking… When you think about it, having a gift can really be a burden.

Same goes for my eyes.

Maybe that's part of the reason a guy with such an outstanding résumé belongs to an obscure organization like the Pretty Boy Detective Club—in which case, presumptuous as it may sound, maybe Yubiwa and I are actually two of a kind, despite seeming to have nothing whatsoever in common on the surface.

Boy, that really does sound presumptuous, doesn't it.

…But the genius of the child genius didn't seem very well suited to gambling, and as I watched him at the slots, he didn't achieve anything worth mentioning: some wins, some losses, just about breaking even, by the looks of it.

I hear that kind of game is designed to be balanced, so basically no one wins big or loses big—apparently, the ideal for the casino is that everyone ends up losing a little bit of money.

Even the guests who lose should go home happy.

As far as I could tell, the Reasonable Doubt had achieved that ideal to some extent—although of course there's the occasional delinquent bossman who ends up throwing away everything he has.

Yeah.

How do I put this? From what I could tell, it all seemed above board—I didn't sense any villainous intent to swindle middle school kids out of every last penny of their allowance.

The guests and staff alike all seemed happy—to the point that the collective satisfaction was rather blinding.

The place felt like one big party.

Since this whole escapade had started with a wad of counterfeit cash, I'd felt scared before we got there, like I was about to enter the underbelly of society. In that sense, the reality was a letdown.

To me, coming to a flashy night spot like this felt like getting lost in a foreign land. I was so uncomfortable that part of me wanted to run away, but another part felt like if everyone else was having fun, what was the problem?

"..
...."

But of course, this was all illegal, right?

The crime of gambling.

The crime of illegally operating a gaming house.

Those were serious violations of the law.

It was all so brazen that it was easy to forget, but if law enforcement showed up here, every last person would get busted.

Dealers and guests alike.

The bunny girls, too.

Management did take some precautions, like banning photography and handing out masks, but that felt perfunctory.

Another thing I'd noticed as I made the rounds was the presence of kids acting as plainclothes security (I say "plainclothes," but of course they were very elegant), though I assume their job was to settle disputes between guests, not to keep out the authorities.

Hmm... It wasn't really my business, but concern (or lack thereof) for the law aside, I couldn't help being a little anxious about their lack of precautionary measures.

Or maybe it *was* my business, since after all, I was part of an undercover investigative team....

"Pardon me, but is everything alright?"

The sudden voice made me jump.

14. Mr. Businessman—Or Rather

I was just taking a little break, which is to say, leaning casually against the wall after having walked around the whole casino—and I hadn't intended to let my guard down, but when I looked over, he was standing right next to me.

Mr. Businessman.

The unforgettable fellow with the slicked-back hair who had set this whole case in motion a few days earlier.

"Ah, uh, um—"

I was obviously and completely flustered.

How could I respond properly to such an unexpected question?

No, unexpected was the wrong word—this was what they call "pre-established harmony," that is, the natural plot line that I should have been expecting and so should have been prepared for. After all, we hadn't come to play around (Mr. Bare-Legs excluded).

We had come to investigate this enigmatic man who had dropped a wad of cash and then given me a tenth of it—and to discover the real reason he had hidden invitations inside those anti-cost-performance counterfeit bills.

So it was actually inevitable that I'd have to confront the man in question at some point tonight—I just hadn't thought I'd be doing it alone, and so directly.

I wasn't prepared for that—which is why I panicked.

But Mr. Businessman paid it no mind.

"My dear sir," he began politely, "you don't seem to be enjoying yourself. Tell me, what might be the problem?"

In fact, he was so excessively polite that I couldn't relax.

"Oh, no, it's not that I'm not enjoying myself…"

Somehow I managed to answer him, however incoherently.

Part of the problem was that since I didn't know his position, I wasn't sure what attitude to take toward him—he'd been very polite to me and his question seemed like something casino management would ask, not to mention the fact that he was wearing a tuxedo, quite unlike the suit he'd had on the other day.

It was almost like he was more dressed up than the dressed-up guests. He gave me the same uneasy feeling as last time, but I still didn't know what was causing it.

"I-It's just, a gi—I mean, a guy like me doesn't really know the rules of these games. I only came with my friends…"

I'd remembered my current appearance just in time to frantically switch the "girl" to "guy."

Right now, I was a pretty boy.

Of course, if I were as mature as the student council president, I probably could have turned it into some sort of elegant joke.

"Your friends? I see." He nodded significantly. "In that case, what would you say to joining me in a nostalgic game of Othello?"

He pointed to a table tucked into one corner of the hall.

It looked to be in some kind of lounge area. I hadn't come across it in my tour of the hall, but when I took a closer look, I saw shogi and go boards laid out on the table—along with the Othello board Mr. Businessman had mentioned.

Okay then.

Even I know how to play Othello.

I'm not an idiot, you know.

"A-And—um, you are…" I asked haltingly.

If I ran after him without a second thought, that would be just as bad as letting him foist the hundred thousand yen (of invitation-stuffed counterfeit bills) on me—so I figured I should at least ask who he was first.

"Oh, how inconsiderate of me," he replied. "My name is Fudatsuki, and I have the good fortune to be the manager and overseer here in famous Kamikazari's Reasonable

Doubt Casino."

"Infamous?"

"I also happen to be the president of the student council—please, follow me."

On that suave note, Mr. Businessmen—er, I mean, student council president?—led me over to the table.

So he wasn't a businessman after all!

He was a middle school student!

That must be why he made me feel uneasy! He wasn't just childlike, he was actually a child! With those thoughts running through my mind, I followed after him—but seriously, a middle school student?

"Heheheh, I wear makeup to make me look more grown-up—a person can turn into anyone they want, you know."

I somehow felt as if he was referring to my boy's getup, and my heart skipped a beat—but after all, I knew a fifth grader who blended in perfectly well with middle school students, so the idea of a middle school student who could pull off a suit or a tuxedo wasn't all that strange… But if he was student council president, did that mean he was in year 3?

"Oh no, I'm in year 2. The old make way for the young nice and early at our school—unlike Yubiwa Academy."

"…"

So he knew that I went to Yubiwa Academy—I guess that made sense, since I'd been wearing a uniform the last time we met.

And he—Fudatsuki—apparently remembered that encounter.

When I thought about the possibility that he'd approached me because he recognized me, I tensed up all over again—I'd been tense to start with, but now I realized that this might not be a simple case of the manager showing concern for a "bored customer."

In which case, I'd better proceed with care.

As a member of the Pretty Boy Detective Club.

…I had no idea how I, the newbie, ended up having to deal head-on with this situation while all the other members got to gamble the night away, but nevertheless, a mission is a mission.

I might have unexpectedly managed to ferret out his name and position, but I still didn't understand his purpose—and I had to find that out.

He ordered a drink from a bunny girl and sat down at the table.

"Black or white, whichever you prefer."

He presented me with the choice like a sommelier offering me a glass of wine, but I honestly didn't care—was there even an advantage to going first or second in Othello? I had a vague idea that going second was better.

"Most likely that's because if you choose to go second, the option arises of placing your disc at a diagonal—while if you go first, it doesn't matter where you place your disc, it's all the same. Which amounts to not having a choice."

What a logical explanation.

Hmm, so that's the situation—but what was I supposed to do with a lecture on Othello?

I chose to go first; that is, I chose black.

If I could get away without agonizing over a choice, then I would.

I'd just kind of gotten swept along into playing this game—even though this was no time to be killing time.

Anyway, the Othello board had the discs built into it.

This wasn't my first time playing the game, but it was my first time with that kind of set.

I'd figured it would be convenient because you can't lose the discs, but now that I was actually using it, I realized how annoying it was to turn the pieces over... Every time I tried to turn a white piece black only to spin it the wrong way and end up with a blank face, I felt slightly irritated.

I just can't keep up with the latest technology.

"So tell me, is something bothering you?"

"Oh, yes, um…"

Even though we went to different schools, we were in the same year, so figured it was fine to use casual language with him, but he was so prim and proper that I was having a hard time finding the right moment to make the switch.

I may be a good-for-nothing human being, but I'm

not the type to get all high-handed with people in the service industry—leaving aside the question of whether what he did was actually part of the service industry, or actually a job at all.

"I-I was just wondering if this was really okay. I mean, outright gambling inside the school… I was worried we might get in trouble with a teacher or something."

That was the mild version.

What I really wanted to say was, "Hey, aren't we gonna get busted by the cops?" (which was still fairly mild), but I couldn't bring myself to be so blunt to the manager himself.

"Heheh, is that what's been bothering you? Rest assured, there's nothing to worry about."

Fudatsuki smiled.

I almost let that smile reassure me, but wait, what was he basing that on? I couldn't let myself blindly swallow his reassurances.

A smile doesn't guarantee anything.

This guy had handed me counterfeit cash.

If I'd used it, I could have gotten in big trouble, and trying to play it off as a joke wouldn't have gotten me off the hook—I would've been committing a crime!

"Why do you say there's nothing to worry about?"

"Tell me, how did you come to grace the halls of our casino?"

If he recognized me, then that was surely a rhetorical

question, but I answered anyway.

I found an invitation inside a counterfeit bill.

"Are there other ways?" I asked.

"Yes, we've taken the liberty of coming up with many ingenious methods of sending out our invitations. We stop at nothing to entertain our guests."

"..."

"A person with the playful spirit to discover that sort of invitation would never report this casino to the police—and so our secret is safe," Fudatsuki pronounced with the utmost confidence.

His argument wasn't so different from saying that everyone here was complicit in the crime—but the phrase "playful spirit" was somehow much more persuasive.

Counterfeit bills as an expression of a playful spirit.

In that case, the Reasonable Doubt Casino itself might also be the product of that same playful spirit.

"...Do you turn a profit?" I asked.

The question might be unsophisticated, but I had to ask—although I did understand his point.

For instance, he ostentatiously drops a million yen, then presents whoever picks it up with a hundred thousand yen containing ten invitations. Any person who figures out that the money is counterfeit, and on top of that that there are invitations inside, has got to be not only sharp and sharp-eyed, but also in some way a kindred spirit.

That person may not be complicit in the crime, but as long as a sense of kinship exists…

…That should allow him to find companions who will "come out and play," although I should add the caveat, "As long as they don't have eyesight like mine." Still, the expense was enormous, and to be blunt, it was wretchedly inefficient.

Even without the cost, I'm sure he could find friends a whole lot faster by advertising online.

The invitations clearly took plenty of time and effort to put together, let alone this gorgeous venue—and while the chips here might cost as much as they did at a real casino, didn't those places make their real profits on the so-called "high rollers"?

As fancy as the place might look, I could hardly imagine that there were any millionaires among the kids gambling here (except the scion of a certain foundation, that is).

"Oh my, you are kind to be concerned for our welfare. Thank you ever so much."

I went and got myself thanked.

Though I wouldn't say I was concerned about them.

"We do indeed turn a profit. This is not my only business venture, you see—and I've been at it a long time."

"Oh…"

So he'd been running other businesses as well, and for a long time? Unbelievable. I'd always thought my neighborhood was peaceful, but now I was starting to wonder if I lived in a den of vice and crime.

"All games, fun and games. Or you could call it investment—after all, job creation is essential."

"Job creation… Speaking of which, is everyone who works here a student at Kamikazari Middle?" I asked, peering around.

There were the dealers, the bunny girls, the plainclothes security.

And they must need people to deliver the beverages, look after the tables, and maintain the slot machines, too.

"Yes, for the most part. Our school has many students with special circumstances—and in any event, it's never too early to learn a trade, is it?"

His speech rang hollow.

To me, working here looked like just another kind of game.

Which was probably a perfectly healthy thing—but given that the whole place was also illegal, I felt like it hardly deserved praise.

Although maybe I only felt that way because I'd discovered the invitations by using the "trick" of looking right through the bills, which meant we'd come here via something of an underhanded route ourselves…

Before I knew it, the Othello board was covered with pieces—about an even split between black and white, so I couldn't tell at a glance who had won.

Huh. Since the pieces were attached to the board, you couldn't just sweep them up into a stack and count them… Yeah, convenience always comes at a cost.

Plus, getting the board back to its starting point at the end of the game took a fair amount of work—I suppose it's a question of personal preference, but I like the standard boards with the loose pieces better.

I bet Michiru the Epicure (who's a neat freak, as it turns out) would definitely prefer this kind of board, though.

Anyhow, since we were playing a game, I figured we should at least figure out who'd won, so I started counting out the pieces, attempting to wrap up our conversation at the same time. "So, when it comes right down to it, I should think of this casino, invitations and all, as a little game of yours?"

With what he'd said about diversified investments and labor-force training, I ended up sounding like some wearisome auditor, but that's why I came here in the first place, so what can you do?

Why was he doing this? To what end? The answer seemed to be, "Because it's fun."

Because it's a game.

It wasn't much, but if that was the only answer, I'd have to accept it—and if you said human beings instinctively love to play, I'd have to nod in agreement.

I guess I should feel satisfied.

But I wasn't so sure the leader would be equally satisfied.

He was Manabu the Aesthete, after all.

Leaving aside the issue of a disregard for profit, I wasn't sure he'd approve of succumbing to the instinctual urge to play with no concern for aesthetics—although experience had already taught me that beautiful mysteries don't necessarily have beautiful solutions.

The score was 33 black to 31 white. I'd won, but by such a narrow margin that I wondered if Fudatsuki hadn't lost on purpose.

Was he just showing me a good time with a nostalgic round of Othello, like he'd promised?

If so, then I felt small for being so fixated on figuring out who'd won—although I couldn't do much about it now.

Anyway, I'd accomplished my goal, so I figured I'd gather up the boys and head out—before the delinquent went bankrupt.

But just as that thought crossed my mind, a bunny girl approached our table.

"Maestro."

She clearly wasn't there to refill our drinks.

"We have a problem."

15. The Problem

The moment I heard those words I had a guess as to what might have happened, but contrary to the first image that popped into my mind, the delinquent hadn't overturned the baccarat table after his losing streak.

In fact, he was leaning against the wall with his head in his hands, wearing a look that said, "I'm screwed! What'll I do about tomorrow's ordering?" Apparently, I was too late to save him from himself.

Actually, I don't know if Michiru the Epicure is personally in charge of ordering provisions, but in any case, he looked like a guy who'd burned through all his cash.

Yes, gambling carries the inherent risk of ruin.

Which reminds me, I'd better state clearly right now that this case file is in no way intended to encourage young people to gamble (your narrator is weak-kneed).

I was curious to know just what kind of loss could transform the aggressive bossman into a depressed shadow of himself in the space of twenty unsupervised minutes, but…hopefully, he could think of today's experience as money well spent on an important life lesson.

It's a cliché, but hotheaded people really are poorly suited to gambling—anyway, that's beside the point.

Fukuroi might have learned a pricey lesson, but from what I could see, the other members of the Pretty Boy Detective Club had paid a fair price for the fun they'd had, and now they were out of chips.

I suppose they saw it more as an arcade than a casino—they all seemed to have won some and lost some in the course of gathering information, then used up the rest of their chips and stepped away from their respective tables once they were done.

All but one of them.

And that one was the problem that the bunny girl had come over to tell Fudatsuki about: Nagahiro Sakiguchi, vice president of the Pretty Boy Detective Club.

Nagahiro the Orator.

"Whoa…" I couldn't help exclaiming as I took in the massive heap of chips stacked on the side table next to him.

And what's more, the chips weren't the same color as the ones he'd originally bought from the purchase booth.

These were definitely not hundred-yen chips.

Each one must have been worth two hundred and fifty, five hundred…maybe even a thousand yen—who knows, some of them might've been worth ten thousand yen a piece!

No way, no freaking way.

One thing was certain, there were a lot of different colors, and the pile as a whole had to represent a serious amount of money.

"Oh man oh man oh man…"

I didn't even need to use my special eyesight.

Anyone could see he was winning big.

Wow, good on us for choosing such a winner to be president of Yubiwa Middle School's student council—but I couldn't bring myself to applaud his success.

In fact, and this might be a bit presumptuous for a regular student like myself, his ostentatious winning streak was so infuriating that a New York gangster voice in my head kept asking, "Whaddaya think yer doin'?" We were supposed to be investigating the casino, and if that meant playing a couple of games in the name of detective work, fine—but what was he thinking, drawing attention to himself like this?

A fox with flowing locks stood out plenty to start with, but now everyone in the casino was looking at him.

The girls, in particular, were transfixed.

Each time Nagahiro the Orator uttered the words "bet," "call," or "raise," the female guests and workers alike flew into a greater frenzy—was that what had brought the bunny girl rushing over to Fudatsuki?

Though maybe she was too late in any case—if

Sakiguchi left the table now, the casino would suffer an enormous loss.

Not enough to bankrupt it, I'm sure, but definitely enough to wipe out the night's earnings.

Didn't he know how to control himself?

With all due respect, this was a guy who'd been student council president since his first year, so maybe he had a greedy streak, or rather a thirst for victory—perhaps he didn't understand the concept of losing gracefully.

Ignoring for a moment the delinquent's miserable defeat, the leader, Mr. Bare-Legs, and the child genius seemed to have no problem at all in that department.

All three stood watching their fellow member's winning streak from afar. The leader looked pleased with his subordinate's performance, Mr. Bare-Legs appeared fed up with the older student's inability to read the room, and the child genius had a blank look on his face that gave no hint whatsoever as to his thoughts.

My own expression was probably most similar to Mr. Bare-Legs'.

Compared to what the vice president was doing, Mr. Bare-Legs amusing himself by sowing panic among his fellow players had been the picture of discretion.

"..."

Worried, I turned back to Fudatsuki, the manager of the casino.

The boy playing Othello with me—or should I call

him the playboy?

Anyway, I was wondering how he'd handle the issue. Was it all just part of the game to him? Would he claim he couldn't care less about taking a loss? Would he let Sakiguchi and the rest of us leave like nothing had happened?

I'm not such a dreamer that I'd genuinely cling to a faint hope like that—after all, if that were his attitude, then the bunny girl would never have interrupted our conversation.

He called this place a casino, so I'm sure he let people take home small winnings without a fuss, but the possessor of that beautiful voice had clearly crossed the line.

The only justification I could think of for that mountain of chips was that he had a young girl to provide for.

And, sure enough, Fudatsuki said, "The student council president."

The hint of a smile played across his face.

He looked at ease, but I took no comfort in his expression—because he'd just said *what*?

The president of Kamikazari Middle School student council had just said—

"The president of the Yubiwa Academy Middle School student council. Is he a friend of yours?"

"…"

Yeah, I guess that would be hard to hide.

These two were the student council presidents of

neighboring, not to mention rival, middle schools—just wearing his hair down when he usually wore it up wasn't much of a disguise. Thinking back to our conversation in the art room, I remembered that a strange look had shadowed Sakiguchi's face when I described "Mr. Businessman."

Not that I had to think too hard—the look had been really obvious.

Sakiguchi had probably known for sure when Kamikazari Middle School came up, or maybe he'd known from the start—the true identity of Mr. Businessman, that is.

Or perhaps I should say the identity of the mastermind behind it all.

"I'm not sure I'd call him my friend… But, um, yes, we're together," I mumbled. "Fellow members, I guess you'd say, or…"

How much of my identity had I given away? He knew I was Sakiguchi's "friend," and no matter how much I played the fool, it was obvious I went to Yubiwa Middle School.

"Heheh," Fudatsuki stood up, apparently finished with me. "You must be concerned about what I plan to do to him."

"C-Concerned, or… Um. Well… I thought you might throw us out…" I sputtered fearfully, although getting thrown out was an optimistic scenario (I'd

111

honestly be happy if we managed to escape the gym in one piece).

"Throw you out? I wouldn't dream of it," Fudatsuki replied as politely as ever. "To the contrary—I'd like to offer the lucky fellow our special service."

16. The Empty Stage

I'd been wondering about it.

The stage between the purchase booth and the cashier's booth—because no matter how much they tried to dress this place up, it was still a school gym, which meant there was a stage, or maybe I should say a platform, and even I, who didn't have an entertainer's bone in my body and couldn't care less about amusing people, thought it was a waste not to put it to some kind of use.

I couldn't help thinking they ought to have some magician or dancer up there, or maybe some kind of video program running—but even though the curtains were up, the stage was empty.

They weren't using it at all.

Fudatsuki could hardly claim he lacked the budget for a stage program, or that he couldn't find a magician or a dancer—who would believe he was short on money when he'd created such a stunning casino?

So even someone as slow on the uptake as I am had

kind of guessed he might be planning to use the stage for something else—and sure enough.

A special program.

"Hahaha!" crowed Sotoin, with whom I'd reconvened. "I chose well when I made him vice president of the Pretty Boy Detective Club, did I not, young Dojima? I predict he will look absolutely gorgeous on stage. Don't you agree?"

Being proud of your subordinates is all well and good, but I'm begging you, please don't go around screaming personal information like "Pretty Boy Detective Club" and "vice president," and definitely not "young Dojima," in an illegal place like this!

Mr. Bare-Legs and the child genius were standing next to us—and the delinquent, too, although he was so dispirited that he looked like a different person.

With four pretty boys together (five, if you included me in my disguise—or no, make that four after all, since the delinquent was for all intents and purposes dead), we made quite a brilliant group, but for once, no one was looking at us.

The eyes of every guest in the casino were trained on the stage—which was no longer empty.

Two men stood on it, facing each other across a table and chairs.

Actually, based on age, I suppose I should say two boys, or to be even more accurate, two pretty boys.

Sakiguchi and Fudatsuki.

As far as looking gorgeous on stage goes, Fudatsuki gave Sakiguchi a run for his money—and while Sakiguchi was a year ahead in school, both held the position of student council president.

"…"

A special program.

The bunny girl who had come over to inform Fudatsuki of the "problem" had explained to me what that meant (it was hard to tell the bunny girls apart, but I was fairly sure she was the same one who had explained the casino to me when we first came in—I guess she must have liked how I looked as a pretty boy, because she was extremely considerate).

Apparently, any guest who won more than a certain amount of money earned the right to a "showdown" with the maestro on stage—and these showdowns were a popular attraction for the casino, or rather, they turned them into spectacles that became the main event of the night.

And of course, they involved gambling.

Would the maestro win, or would the chosen gambler win? That was the question, but the odds were drastically out of balance.

Fudatsuki, it seemed, had never once lost one of these special programs—so the spectacle wasn't so much about who would win as whether he could keep his winning streak going.

No, that wasn't it either.

The power of his winning streak was itself the show—which is to say, it seemed more about putting a spell on the audience than selling them on another visit.

In which case, I could probably assume he'd handed me that narrow victory in Othello earlier.

The flip side was that if the challenger did manage to win, Fudatsuki faced a devastating loss—so naturally, most people bet against him, because the odds on him were scarcely better than 1:1.

And that wasn't all.

The rules stated that the challenger was to place all his chips above a certain set amount on the table—so if he lost, he'd lose them all (like a certain delinquent I know).

I didn't say this to the nice bunny girl, but the deal was simple. This show wasn't about entertaining the guests. It wasn't even about winning back the casino's losses—it was about profit. The casino stood to take in both the one guest's excessive winnings and everything the other guests wagered on him.

A brilliant system, you might say.

Or a dishonest one?

No, when I thought about the risk Fudatsuki—that is, the casino—was taking on, the system didn't necessarily strike me as dirty... If Fudatsuki lost, then his opponent (in this case Sakiguchi) wouldn't just get three times or even ten times the chips he'd bet.

He'd get everything.

The right to run the casino would be transferred to the winner—which meant that while Sakiguchi was betting unearned money, the casino was staking its own destruction.

Not to bring up cost performance again, but no one could put on a show like this without the kind of absolute confidence that goes beyond any calculation of profit and loss.

Absolute confidence.

Or should I say, absolute playfulness.

As I was drifting around trying to get a sense of the place, the situation had taken an unexpected turn—and now all I could do was watch the showdown between the two student council presidents with my heart in my throat.

Though strictly speaking, Sakiguchi could have turned down his role in this show—he wasn't obligated to get up on stage.

When the staff approached him, he could have firmly refused in that beautiful voice of his—but as the bunny girl declared, no one in the history of the casino had ever turned down the invitation.

Was it greed that motivated them? I don't think so.

I'm sure there are some gamblers who simply couldn't say no to the right and opportunity to face down the legendary maestro—but I doubt that was the only reason people accepted Fudatsuki's proposition.

In a calmer environment, I'm certain most people would decide to keep the money they'd won through luck or skill—and at first glance, it struck me as strange that not a single person had turned down Fudatsuki's offer. But that's the magnetism and magic of the casino.

I mean, before being invited up to the stage, the challenger was surrounded by bunny girls, praised to the skies, introduced to the crowd as a winner, and generally treated like a star—so you can imagine how hard it would be, in that overpowering atmosphere, to say, "No, I'd prefer to skip the big showdown."

I suppose it's what they call reading the room.

To give a more familiar example, when your whole class is voting yes, it's tough to be the only one to vote no—and in the same way, once the challengers get swept up in that atmosphere, they start to think, "Oh well, it was easy money anyway, might as well give it a go."

A very well-thought-out system…

Or more like a con, and a polished one at that.

"Ahem! There's nothing to worry about, young Dojima! Just relax."

Sotoin rested a hand on my shoulder.

I'm sure he intended it to be soothing.

But unlike when Fudatsuki said those words, now they had the opposite effect of making me deeply anxious.

"Nagahiro is certainly not the kind of person to lose

his head and be swept up onto the stage—he got up there of his own free will. He's fully aware of what he's doing!"

"Um…"

I wasn't sure what to think.

"Totally, we all trust him when it comes to that. Naga-hiro isn't gonna lose his grip just 'cause he's surrounded by a bunch of bunny girls," Mr. Bare-Legs concurred, his hands intertwined behind his head and his legs crossed even though he was standing up. "Unless they're still lit-tle," he added.

"…"

Can you really call that trust?

Personally, I'd call it suspicion.

But when I looked back up at the stage, it was just like they'd said—Sakiguchi the master speaker, guide (or goad, depending on how you look at it) of the peo-ple, didn't look at all like he'd been pulled up to the stage against his will, a victim of the frenzied atmosphere in the room.

So did he have a reason for going up there?

A reason, or, an objective?

Could he have been planning this from the start, hence his insane winning streak? Had he anticipated the existence of a special program based solely on the pres-ence of an empty stage?

At that point, we'd be talking more intuition than de-duction.

Maybe I was reading too much into it, but if he'd thought of Kamikazari Middle's student council president when he heard my story about the dropped cash, then it did seem possible…

I just didn't know.

But one thing seemed certain: the vice president of the Pretty Boy Detective Club was on stage to carry out some sort of detective work.

"Oh, and young Dojima—since your eyesight will not affect the outcome of this game, feel free to place a bet," Sotoin said, as if he'd just remembered, but the timing was all wrong.

I wasn't inclined to go along with the frenzied mood of the casino hall.

I'd rather sit this one out.

"…By the way, who did you put your money on?" I asked the three Pretty Boys who had headed over to the purchase booth once again to buy more chips—which is to say, all of them except the delinquent, who had gotten a head start on emptying his purse.

"Ten on the manager to win."

"Ten on the guy with the slicked-back hair."

The child genius pointed silently to Fudatsuki.

All three had unexpectedly gone with the safe bet.

17. The Special Program

"Ladies and gentlemen! At long last, I have the pleasure of announcing another installment of our special program! Let the games begin!"

An exceedingly cheerful bunny girl, mic in hand, announced this to the room as she hopped around the stage like a veritable rabbit—the same bunny girl, incidentally, who had treated me so kindly (I was finally starting to recognize her face).

After briefly introducing the two players, she briskly explained how the show would proceed.

Compared to the explanation she'd given me earlier, this version was more of a performance, but I was starting to realize she had a flair for exposition and elucidation—maybe that was why she'd been given the job of MC?

According to the explanation she gave from the stage, Sakiguchi, the "challenger," was free to choose whatever game he wanted. Of course, his choices were limited to the games offered in the casino, but from the audience's perspective, this seemed like a huge concession in his favor.

I suppose that impression may have stemmed from a lack of knowledge about casino games, though—maybe they don't really involve skill or advantage at all.

Anyway, naturally enough, Sakiguchi selected poker.

The game at which he'd racked up such massive winnings, earning him the right to challenge the maestro.

Maybe he was getting superstitious.

"…"

"…"

Huh?

The two players appeared to exchange some words across the table—but since they weren't wearing mics, the audience couldn't hear what they said. The fact that the music was cranked up to full volume to rev up the mood didn't help, either.

If I took off my glasses, I might have been able to read their lips—or not, since I don't actually know how to read lips.

Just because I can see the stars doesn't mean I know the name of every constellation—it sounds obvious, but if you want skills, you've got to acquire them.

Still, from what I could tell at a distance with my normal vision, this didn't seem to be their first encounter—and though they both smiled as they spoke, there didn't seem to be a shred of friendly feeling between them.

"Hey, do you guys know him?" I asked no one in particular.

The delinquent, who seemed to have recovered by that point, was the one who replied. "Just his name—he's the president of Kamikazari's student council. I hear he's a shrewd one, unlike our councilman, but I gotta say I'm surprised he's running an underground operation like this. As surprised as I am when people say, 'Whales are almost as smart as humans, so you shouldn't eat them.' Almost as smart as humans? Well that ain't so smart, is it."

If the satire was back, then he must be okay.

When it came to food-related issues, Michiru the Epicure apparently had some strong opinions.

"Saying you shouldn't eat them because they're cute would be closer to the truth. They may not have legs, but they sure have nice tail fins," declared Mr. Bare-Legs, who was a bit too hung up on legs for his own good.

"And by the way, I don't know the guy," he added. "But after today, my opinion of Kamikazari Middle has really improved. Wonder if the student council president has made some reforms."

"Hahaha." Sotoin just laughed loudly.

Apparently, he had neither information to share nor deductions to offer.

I was used to that by now, so it didn't bother me.

I figured I could find out more about the relationship between the two student council presidents later by asking our councilman. He'd leapt onto the stage before he could explain anything—and now the game was about to begin.

The bunny girl climbed down from the stage, leaving only the two players and the dealer.

The chairs had been arranged so we couldn't see the faces of the five cards dealt to each of them, probably to raise the suspense level for the audience—or maybe because if we could see them, the players would be able to guess one another's hands from our reactions.

In which case, both the contestants and the viewers would probably lose interest in the big showdown.

Each player started with thirty chips, and the game was to continue until one or the other went bust. The ante was one chip, they could trade in cards once per game and each raise once, and neither could bet more than the other player currently had.

… I say that like some expert, but actually I'm not just parroting the bunny girl's words, I'm parrying them—I know zilch about the rules of poker.

I don't even know what all the hands are, let alone which are stronger than which—I've heard the phrase "royal flush," but I don't have a clue what that actually is.

My ignorance isn't even about poker or blackjack or baccarat specifically. I don't have friends, so I've just never really played cards much.

I don't get why an ace (1) is stronger than a king

(13)—and I sense some sexism in the fact that the king is better than the queen.

Although that may ring a bit false coming from a girl dressed up as a boy.

"Hmph. Don't ask me. Maybe the king is protecting the queen by taking unlucky number 13," said the delinquent, introducing his own twisted version of "ladies first."

I was just thinking how delighted I was to see this sign of his full recovery when he added, "Shit, if I had any money left, I'd bet it all on Nagahiro."

What sort of nonsense was that! Clearly, he hadn't learned anything from his mistakes.

Learn your lesson already!

"Stop being stupid, Dojima. If I bet a hundred on Nagahiro right now, I could win back every damn yen I lost tonight."

Apparently, the delinquent was almost as smart as a whale.

The music changed. They must have a sound guy back there somewhere.

Just how many people were involved in running this casino? I didn't even think Kamikazari Middle had that many students.

The music was so loud that the players on stage didn't seem able to hear each other anymore, so they'd resorted to hand gestures like tapping the table to indicate when they wanted to trade in cards, bet, or raise.

A novice like me couldn't understand much of what was going on, but judging from the excitement of the crowd, the game must have gotten off to a thrilling start.

"…What just happened?"

"Hahaha. Nagahiro seems to have set an unexpected trap. Although I have no idea what it might consist of," the leader said with a bold smile.

"Was it that unusual?"

"Who knows? I don't know the rules of poker, so I wouldn't understand anyway."

You don't know either, eh?

Then why do you look so bold?

"Unfortunately, you see, only my eye is trained. Not my mind."

"…Is that why you chose blackjack? Because the rules of blackjack are aesthetically pleasing?"

"Oh no, I don't really understand blackjack either—I've just memorized a few strong hands for blackjack and poker. That's my secret to success."

"…"

Um, what did that mean, exactly?

He only knew strong hands, so therefore he was a strong player?

That was a strategy?

While I was busy trying to pick my jaw up off the floor, the first game seemed to have come to an end—and the chips were pushed from the center of the table toward Sakiguchi.

The crowd went wild.

I couldn't keep up.

Sotoin, on the other hand, was keeping up just fine, or rather, taking the lead by pumping his fist in the air, but it was already obvious that his excitement wasn't based on much more knowledge than I had.

Maybe he was just happy about his fellow club member's success, but in that case, why hadn't he bet on Sakiguchi to win?

Sakiguchi won the second game, too (I think)—was he going to sweep the whole match just like that, and add casino manager to his résumé alongside student council president and club VP? I worried that if that happened, he'd have too many titles (oh, the things I worry about), but then Fudatsuki won the third game (as far as I could tell).

It was now two games to one, but the division of chips had basically gone back to where it started—so perhaps we were witnessing a well-matched tug of war?

As it turned out, that pattern continued.

A big win, a little loss, a big loss, a little win, a sudden windfall, immediately reversed…

Maybe this is simply what better bettors do, but as a novice, I couldn't help feeling a little bored by the long back-and-forth with no end in sight.

Contrary to the mood of the ever-more-excited crowd, I was starting to think about slipping away to the lounge for a drink.

And that was when the incident occurred.

18. The Stagehand

The incident.

Or perhaps I should say the accident.

Also, I don't think it exactly "happened" right then—it had been "happening" all along. I just happened to realize it was happening at that moment.

I, and only I.

Realized, or rather, saw.

…While our comrade the councilman was locked in battle over some large sum of money whose exact sum I didn't know, I (pardon me for talking about myself so much) couldn't keep my mind from wandering as the game dragged on—to be specific, it was my glasses.

The glasses that I wear to protect, rather than correct, my vision—broadly speaking, I suppose they fall into the same category as sunglasses, but anyway, the point is, they're a type of protection. Armor, if you will.

So I ought to be grateful for them and not depressed about having to wear them, but still, glasses are glasses, and after I've had them on for a while, my ears and nose start to get sore—and sometimes I just want a break.

Which is why I took them off, just for a second—although in retrospect, that was a careless act on my part.

Earlier, the leader had told me I could throw down a side bet if I wanted to, but it was still problematic for me—a person unquestionably on Sakiguchi's side—to employ my preternatural vision as I watched from the floor.

That's because I was able to see through the cards in Fudatsuki's hand, which only he was supposed to be able to see—and theoretically, I could have used some sort of sign to communicate the content of his hand to Sakiguchi.

In other words, we could have cheated.

Which means that no matter how bored I was by the game (sorry), I shouldn't have taken off my glasses in the middle—but.

What I saw when I took them off this time wasn't the inside of Fudatsuki's cards—well, I did vaguely see that, too, but I saw something else even more clearly.

Something, or rather…

Someone.

There should only have been three people on stage—Sakiguchi the challenger and Fudatsuki the reigning champion, plus the dealer—but at some point, *a fourth person had joined them.*

At what point?

Probably before the show even started.

I mean, I can't imagine this fourth person was waiting for me to take my glasses off before coming on stage—and needless to say, we weren't talking about a bunny girl here.

To the contrary, in contrast to the eminently visible bunnies, this was a "kuroko": a black-clad stagehand.

Performance is performance, but this was the kind of stagehand you see in traditional puppet theatre, not casino shows—not like I've ever been to a puppet theatre performance, but even I (or anyone for that matter) should know about kuroko.

They do share one thing with the bunny girls, though—their all-black outfits.

Their faces, bodies, hands, and feet are wrapped in cloth—you could call it a full-body dress code meant to symbolize absence or invisibility.

The thing is, this kuroko was present.

And visible. To me, anyway.

"…"

Unable to fully hide my confusion, I looked around—observing not only the members of the Pretty Boy Detective Club but the entire audience, which was still going wild over the tug-of-war on stage, with the full powers of my "vision."

Not a single person seemed aware of the fourth

person on the stage, however—I could tell because none of their gazes were trained on the kuroko.

…Was I the only one who could see this other figure?

Was the kuroko like a ghost—as invisible as air?

Still confused, I looked back at the stage. The issue wasn't just the presence but the *location* of the kuroko.

He—or maybe she? I'd assumed it was a boy based on the silhouette, but I myself was evidence that such things could be misleading—anyway, he or she was standing directly behind Sakiguchi.

The kuroko's position was that of a guardian angel, although of course an angel would be hovering rather than standing, but in any case, no matter how carefully I choose my words so as not to be accused of slander based purely on assumption, the fact is that the kuroko was peering over Sakiguchi's shoulder at his cards.

And not just that.

After peering at them, the kuroko was signaling—with silent hand gestures—to Fudatsuki where he was seated across the table from Sakiguchi.

I don't possess the brilliant insight to have actually deciphered the signs, but naturally, it wasn't hard to figure out that they were meant to communicate the content of Sakiguchi's hand.

In other words, the kuroko was telling Fudatsuki what cards his opponent held—and Fudatsuki was using that information to decide whether he should bet or fold.

It was the only possible conclusion.

I'm sure it wasn't quite that simple—Fudatsuki wasn't necessarily winning every game, and actually, if you went by number of wins alone, Sakiguchi was ahead.

But even with fewer wins, Fudatsuki seemed to have the upper hand whenever a lot of chips were at stake, and in that regard, I had to conclude that he was able to see through Sakiguchi's bluffs.

See through, or rather, see from behind—which meant that what looked like a close tug-of-war between the two players was really no more than judicious manipulation on the part of the maestro.

Meant to excite the audience.

Which doesn't sound so bad, when you put it that way, but in truth the game was rigged—because when you know your opponent's hand, you can manipulate him however you want.

It was probably far easier than engineering that close game of Othello with me earlier.

"Um…"

I brought my hand to my chin, and considered the situation like a detective.

An undefeated overseer with an unbroken winning streak?

A desperate gamble, bringing guests who won too much on stage and then betting everything?

A momentous showdown, with the casino itself on

the line?

But with a kuroko employed to peek at the challenger's cards… I put my glasses back on.

The kuroko vanished.

All I saw was the back wall of the stage.

Just like "Mr. Businessman," aka Fudatsuki, had vanished on the morning he dropped a million yen—vanished and was gone.

I shifted my glasses down my nose.

The kuroko reappeared.

I pushed them back up.

The figure disappeared.

…I didn't get it.

This wasn't just beyond my powers of imagination, it was beyond the bounds of human knowledge.

Still, there was one thing I could say with complete certainty—and after taking a long, deep breath, I yelled it at the top of my lungs.

"This is a scam!"

19. Defeat

"This is a scam!"

No sooner had I screamed those words than I felt something being stuffed into my mouth, forcibly silencing me—I panicked for a second about what that something might be, but it turned out to be Fukuroi's right hand.

Really?

Michiru the Epicure was kind enough to let me eat his own hand?

I'd be lying if I said it was delicious—but in the sense that I wanted to spit it out in surprise, it was indeed similar to his other culinary creations.

"Ermph! Ergh, ermph!"

"Calm down, you idiot," the delinquent hissed. "Think about where you are."

"B-But, Delinquent!"

"Delinquent?"

He glared at me.

Crap. I'd blurted out my secret nickname for him—apparently my tongue had slipped because he'd twisted it around by stuffing his hand into my mouth.

"So that's what you think of me, is it, kid?"

"Th-This is no time for a question like that!" I snapped back. At the bossman.

I may have good vision, but that doesn't mean I look before I leap.

"I-It really is a scam! You might not be able to see it, Deli—Fukuroi, but I can. I swear…"

"I get it, I get it. I'm not questioning that. No one's saying you're lying. But," he lowered his voice as he glanced around, "there's no point in screaming it at the top of your lungs in the middle of this nest of vipers."

He was right.

It wasn't just pointless, it was downright dangerous.

I was the only one with special eyesight, and it would have been tough to prove my claim—because only I can see the things that only I can see.

No matter how much I insisted a mysterious kuro-ko was on stage communicating secretly with Fudatsuki, if no one in the audience could see this kuroko, they'd write me off as tragically delusional, and the management would toss me out for making false accusations.

I know, because I spent ten years chasing a star only I could see—I know very well that my claims can't be trusted.

Only five people have ever believed me.

These five pretty boys.

…So while I had to grudgingly admit that Fukuroi was right, something about the way he said it bothered me.

A nest of vipers.

…Did he see all these people as enemies?

I mean, given the amount of money he'd just squandered, it made sense, but I had a feeling that wasn't the whole story.

"Hey, look! The guy with the lolicon is going all in!"

A guy with a lolicon going all in?

Now that sounds like serious trouble, I thought, turning back toward the stage. I guess Fukuroi was the only one who'd heard me shout, because Mr. Bare-Legs, the leader, and the child genius were all watching the show just like before.

Sakiguchi must've been dealt a good hand, because he'd just bet all his chips.

"Aha. Staking it all, how beautiful," murmured the possessor of the refined aesthetic.

Refined but dangerous.

It was dangerous to begin with, but now… I shifted my glasses down and looked at the stage again.

"Hm? What is it, young Dojima? I notice you've been fidgeting with your glasses for the past few minutes. Are you playing some sort of joke?"

The president of this detective club isn't the sharpest tool in the shed.

I don't have that kind of time to waste.

Anyway—this is what I saw:

I saw Sakiguchi's winning hand (the numbers were in sequence, which I'm guessing is good), and the kuroko looking over his shoulder.

I saw the kuroko give the sign, and Fudatsuki receive it—and I felt like I could even see him secretly gloating inside.

He remained silent for a moment after Sakiguchi bet all his chips, then pushed his chips into the center of the table as well.

The audience's roar reached fever pitch, but the outcome was already obvious.

Pre-established harmony.

I don't know much about poker hands, but when the two of them showed their cards, it was obvious which was better.

To cut to the chase, tonight's special program once again ended in victory for the maestro—extending his winning streak yet again.

The Reasonable Doubt Casino not only recouped a mountain of chips from the guest who'd won big, but it also raked in all the money the audience had bet on this "challenger," which made for a huge profit—and if I must tell the sad story in its entirety.

The leader, Mr. Bare-Legs, and the child genius each succeeded in turning the thousand yen they'd bet on Fu-datsuki into a thousand and one.

20. A Temporary Retreat

"Thank you very much. We hope to have the pleasure of your custom again in the future—it has been an honor to host the illustrious members of the Pretty Boy Detective Club."

With that polite farewell straight from the mouth of the maestro, we returned to the art room at Yubiwa Academy.

Although we'd succeeded to some extent in our secret investigation en route to that ignominious exit, it felt more like a rout than a job well done.

At least, it would be mighty difficult to consider the phone number that the kind bunny girl slipped into my hand as we were leaving a full success.

The delinquent had suffered a particularly devastating loss, what with blowing all his cash, but the other members had each lost their thousand yen, too (if you did the math, they were actually only nine hundred and ninety-nine yen in the hole), and Sakiguchi had been humiliated on stage in front of a full house.

Of course, considering the age of his fiancée, life itself might be a humiliation for him, but that doesn't mean an additional layer of shame would have no impact—and as his fellow club member, I couldn't help being furious.

If he'd lost fair and square, I could have brushed it off as the risk inherent in games and gambling, but this was far from fair and square.

It was a scam.

If Fudatsuki had used the card-peeking to engineer a fair, fifty-fifty fight for the sake of a good show, I could maaaybe accept that. But all the ups and downs had led to a massive haul for the casino.

Their profits were huge.

Simply put, they were playing dirty.

Such unfairness made the words "playful spirit" ring hollow—and made the gorgeous, even hedonistic casino look like nothing more than a flimsy, ostentatious veneer.

Fudatsuki made pretty speeches, but I guess in the end all he cared about was profit.

I wanted to give up.

I felt like they were using, even exploiting, people's playful spirit—and I had to face the fact that the million-yen bundle of cash had held none of the boyish spirit or aesthetic excellence we'd initially seen in it.

…But questions still remained.

By beating Sakiguchi in the winner-take-all onstage

showdown, the casino had avoided losing money and made some extra profit from the crowd, but not even that seemed like enough to cover the expense of such an over-the-top establishment.

Sure, they probably saved some money on rent by using the school gym… But the electricity bill from the slot machines alone must be huge.

And more than anything, who was that kuroko?

If they had a veritable "Invisible Man" on staff, the casino couldn't lose—and it wasn't just the onstage show; the kuroko could get involved in all the games.

I happened to take my glasses off at that moment, but if I'd had them off from the start, I might have seen the black figure acting in secret all over the casino.

Chance or luck had nothing to do with it.

Fudatsuki could engineer all the amusing games and hair-raising, pulse-pounding showdowns he wanted.

He could hook his guests on gambling far more deeply than a normal casino.

He could probably do whatever he wanted.

But the very idea of an invisible kuroko wandering the casino smacked of fantasy—something that belonged in a sci-fi story, not a mystery novel.

Kurokos of the theater world succeed on the basis of a tacit agreement with the audience that they're "invisible" or "nonexistent"—in other words, even though they're visible, the audience pretends they're not.

But not this one.

No doubt about it, this kuroko really was invisible—to everyone but me.

When I checked with the other members of the club, it wasn't just Fukuroi: Mr. Bare-Legs, the child genius, the leader—not to mention Sakiguchi, the one whose cards were being spied on—all confirmed that they hadn't seen the kuroko.

"Hahaha. It's exactly like the Emperor's New Clothes!" Sotoin exclaimed, sinking into the art room sofa. "The kuroko was wearing invisible clothes, I assume? And our young Dojima was the only one sharp enough to see through the farce and call out, 'The emperor is naked!'—she hasn't lost the innocent heart of a young boy!"

I blushed.

Did that mean I fulfilled Rule #2 of the Pretty Boy Detective Club (Be a boy)?

But even if the kuroko had been wearing "invisible clothes," I still hadn't been able to see the person underneath.

"By the way," the delinquent said, setting our tea and supper of yakisoba on the table. "In the original version of the Emperor's New Clothes, after the kid points out that the emperor is naked, the parade continues. So even though he's right, everyone ignores him because he's a kid, and because he's in the minority. Pretty damn thought-provoking for a children's story, if you ask me."

Huh, I never knew that.

The delinquent is surprisingly cultured.

Or maybe that's just basic knowledge for a satirist who can whip up a pan of yakisoba in the blink of an eye.

Anyway, I don't exactly view myself as an innocent child—and if a boyish heart was what it took to see the kuroko's clothes, then it should have been the other members of the Pretty Boy Detective Club who saw them, not a twisted individual like me.

Which meant this wasn't an abstract question of attitude.

This person was physically invisible—like a puff of air, in a very real sense.

Actually, no.

There was nothing physical or real about it—who could have imagined I'd see something like that?

"Well, to tell you the truth..." Just then, Sakiguchi interrupted my thoughts. "I knew from the start—and I was expecting something like this to happen."

"..."

I couldn't help looking at our eminently worthy student council president with more doubt than ever before—who would actually say something like that?

Although I'll admit that his comment *was* rather detective-like.

Still, for someone who'd suffered such total defeat on stage, it couldn't even pass as sour grapes.

It seemed all the more flagrantly ridiculous coming from such a beautiful boy—but then again, even when he suffered that humiliating defeat in front of all those people and lost every last chip he'd racked up, and even when he was escorted out of the building by the student council president of Kamikazari Middle (whom he seemed to know), he didn't appear the least bit shaken or dismayed.

He accepted his defeat calmly, stood up, and leisurely departed the stage—I'll admit I'm biased, but I think anyone would say he lost gracefully.

So gracefully, in fact, that it seemed unnatural. But if he'd been expecting to lose all along, then his unnatural attitude made more sense.

He must have planned it all out—from his sweep of the poker tables to his appearance on stage.

"Oho. You seem to have some thoughts on this matter, Nagahiro. Pray tell us what they are," the leader urged with a grin.

Yes, his attitude was generous, but it also meant he had no concept of what his subordinates were getting up to—honestly, what the hell kind of leadership is that?

The information-sharing protocol in this organization was totally non-functional.

It struck me as a bit fishy, but come to think of it, Sakiguchi had taken the initiative on an independent investigation last time, too—and Yubiwa had helped him out. I glanced over at the child genius.

His face was blank as always.

Impressive that he could eat yakisoba this delicious without losing his deadpan demeanor.

By the way, if you're wondering about Mr. Bare-Legs, he'd burrowed into the bed and passed out in his clothes the instant we got back to the art room (yes, there's a bed in the art room. With a canopy)—apparently, he'd had too much fun and tuckered himself out.

Maybe he needs more rest than the ordinary middle school student because he's so active. And he does look like a regular angel when he's sleeping.

Meanwhile, the eyes of Sotoin the fifth grader were sparkling with excitement, like he simply could not wait to hear what Sakiguchi had to say.

This kid gets excited about everything.

"With pleasure. But where to begin?" the councilman mused in a troubled tone. "I find myself regretting that I didn't inform you of this when Ms. Dojima first told us about her encounter."

"Hmph. You said it, Nagahiro. If you'd told us then, I wouldn'ta burned through all my cash."

It was a delinquent-worthy accusation, but it was just an excuse—he had to take responsibility for his own losses.

"Delinquent debt," I muttered, but everyone ignored me.

Strange, I could have sworn *I* wasn't invisible…

Anyway, the delinquent went on undisturbed. "I don't get complicated explanations, okay? So start at the beginning and tell us everything in order," he commanded.

"Yes, I suppose that may be the only way." The vice president of the Pretty Boy Detective Club shrugged reluctantly. "Ladies and gentlemen," he began in his customary beautiful voice, to which I was by now so well accustomed.

21. Investigation Report

"Ladies and gentlemen.

"I did not conduct the investigation which I am about to discuss in my capacity as a member of the Pretty Boy Detective Club, but rather as president of the Yubiwa Middle School student council—my aim was to maintain the peace, or perhaps one might say to establish public order.

"There was a community connection as well.

"In short, I had been hearing rumors about Kamikazari Middle School for quite some time—vague rumors about unsavory activities taking place there.

"Kamikazari is located a bit too close for me to simply dismiss it as another school's business; I could not ignore the problem.

"Neither could I guarantee that the students of Yubiwa Academy would suffer no negative impact—and so I decided I must take preventive measures.

"As student council president, I have a responsibility

to protect the students of our school.

"I had been looking into the matter for some time, but with limited success—I sensed very strongly that the students at Kamikazari Middle were putting up a united front. None would talk, which was naturally incomprehensible to a person like me, whose only strength lies in speech.

"No matter how persistently I pursued the rumors, the trail inevitably fizzled out. To be frank, I was at my wit's end.

"Of course, since our schools are rivals, students no doubt felt especially reluctant to leak information to me... Their silence was more or less monolithic.

"Yet Kamikazari Middle was not always like that—when I was a first-year student, it was a much freer, more open place, for both better and worse.

"And it only became such a tightly controlled school, for both better and worse, after he enrolled.

"He.

"Yes, Fudatsuki—while he has only recently become student council president, his influence, or perhaps I should say his charisma, has been operating since he entered the school.

"He stood out more brilliantly even than I, it seems.

"And we might just as well call his charisma what it is: business acumen—because despite being a middle school student, he has launched a series of ventures with

Kamikazari students as his staff.

"The casino may be the most emblematic of these ventures, but there seem to be many others, as well—although their nature remains a mystery.

"Here at our school we have a child genius involved in running a foundation, but Fudatsuki's gift is different—in the blink of an eye, he had Kamikazari Middle under his thumb.

"Saying he did it with the power of money has a nasty ring to it.

"But there is no question that Fudatsuki brought a certain order to Kamikazari Middle—and I naturally must credit him for the achievement.

"Nevertheless, as the student council president of a neighboring school, I saw his skill as a threat—because his actions were by no means those of a moderate.

"As Ms. Dojima has already guessed, he and I had crossed paths in our capacity as student council presidents—and so I knew what kind of person he was.

"Appearances to the contrary, he is intensely ambitious.

"Make no mistake, he is not the type to be satisfied controlling the affairs of his own school alone—and I feared he would soon move to seize control of others.

"They call him 'maestro.'

"A fitting title indeed, for one who aspires to be master of all he surveys.

"These are the reasons that I, as student council president, had begun taking preventive measures—though without much success, as I mentioned a moment ago.

"In all honesty, I did not know what Fudatsuki was doing or planning—but when I heard Ms. Dojima describe her 'Mr. Businessman' the other day, I sensed the critical moment had arrived.

"Fudatsuki, it seemed, had finally set his nefarious sights on Yubiwa Academy."

22. Turf War

About that boundary line between Yubiwa Academy and Kamikazari Middle School.

We'd crossed it to visit the Reasonable Doubt Casino, but from the opposite perspective, you could just as well invade Yubiwa Academy's territory from the Kamikazari side.

In fact, that's precisely what Fudatsuki was doing when I saw him on my way to school—he was using that counterfeit million yen as literal groundbait to lure Yubiwa Academy students to his casino.

Oh so carelessly.

And you could say he hooked me—if I hadn't seen the kuroko, my impression of Kamikazari would probably have changed for the better.

I'd be lying if I said Fudatsuki hadn't charmed me when he so politely offered me a game of Othello, standing around twiddling my thumbs as I was—and I'm sure he looked really cool to everyone else when he was up there on the stage, winning big.

As long as they didn't know the trick—yes, the trick.

"...I understand about Fudatsuki—but Sakiguchi..."
I began.

I now understood the connection between the two student council presidents, and why Sakiguchi had approached Kamikazari Middle School with ulterior motives in the first place—but neither was my real concern.

What I really wanted to understand was the trick—that is, the presence of the kuroko.

Or rather, the absence.

"What should we make of that?"

Given that he wasn't able to see the figure, he couldn't have predicted it, could he? He wouldn't have lost like that if he knew about the kuroko, right?

"No, I predicted that, too," he nodded. "I can only wish that I hadn't—but all my precautions had no effect, and the situation only got progressively worse. However..."

Sakiguchi looked over at the leader.

Sotoin tilted his head, looking perplexed.

How can he always guess what the blank-faced child genius is thinking yet be so bad at picking up on this kind of explanation? I'm beginning to wonder if our fifth-grade Kogoro is really suited to being the world's greatest detective.

Inevitably (I'm sorry to say), Sakiguchi picked up the

thread of his own trailing sentence.

"However, the answer to your question is the concern of the Pretty Boy Detective Club, not the Yubiwa Academy student council—Ms. Dojima, do you remember the Twenties?"

23. The Twenties

"The Twenties?! Did the guy with the lolicon just say the Twenties?!" Mr. Bare-Legs broke in, leaping up in response to Sakiguchi's mellifluous voice.

Whether it was thanks to the quality of the bedsprings or because his legs are that powerful even in a reclining position, he literally sprang to his feet—a reaction so excessive that I half wondered if he'd bust through the canopy like some cartoon character.

"I did say 'the Twenties,' but I don't have a lolicon," Mr. Lolicon countered curtly.

"Never mind that, you did say 'the Twenties'!" Mr. Bare-Legs shouted, instantly shaking off all signs of sleepiness as he raced over to Sakiguchi with incredible, and unnecessary, speed.

But maybe his reaction wasn't excessive after all.

Since during the Pretty Boy Detective Club's last tangle with the organization in question, it was Mr. Bare-Legs—angel on the surface, physical dynamo underneath—who laid his life on the line more than any of us, and it would come as no surprise if that experience had traumatized him.

The Twenties.

I don't even know how to properly describe them—but basically, they're a criminal organization.

A bona fide criminal organization, though you'd never guess it from that poppy name of theirs, which makes them sound like a baseball team or something—and they'd kidnapped Sotoin and me with unimaginable aplomb.

Mr. Bare-Legs had fallen into their clutches as well, in his attempt to rescue us—but if that experience was etched into his mind…

"So, then, I get to see Rei again?! That gorgeous woman?! The one with the revealing outfits?! The Rei-vishing Beauty with Twenty Faces?!"

…There was no sign of any emotional scarring as he leaned forward eagerly and inquired about his erstwhile captor. Well, I suppose that level of victimization might not inflict much trauma on a guy who'd been kidnapped three times already.

To the contrary, the enemy's ringleader had stolen his heart.

Though I have to admit she's the kind of jaw-dropping beauty who could put just about any guy under her spell…

"No, you will not get to see her," Sakiguchi scolded him sharply—and with impressive rationality. He, at least, was apparently immune to the charms of jaw-dropping leaders of criminal organizations.

Or maybe that was his standard stance with regard to older women?

"That would not be a desirable outcome," he continued, "which is why I've been attempting to devise a strategy that allows us to avoid any further contact with her organization."

"Oh," Mr. Bare-Legs muttered, losing interest immediately.

But instead of returning to the bed, he sat down on the sofa, snatched the plate of yakisoba the child genius had been in the middle of eating, and began scarfing it down without so much as a by-your-leave.

What a free spirit.

"Then I won't get to see those voluptuous legs again? Just because you prefer slender legs—"

"I most certainly do not prefer slender legs. The legs of the young lady my parents selected as my fiancée just happen to be slender, that's all."

If you ask me, that explanation just happened to be rather suspicious… So suspicious, in fact, that if I had a cell phone, I'd have reported him to the police immediately.

But maybe since Sakiguchi is closer to a criminal than

any of us, he's also more hostile toward other criminals, and more likely to take the moral high ground—in fact, our leader Sotoin had made some comments that suggested he wasn't entirely disapproving of Rei himself.

Which was perhaps what motivated his next words.

"Ahem. Nagahiro, do tell. How are the Twenties involved with the casino?" he asked with interest—although our boundlessly curious leader seems interested in just about everything.

"I'll explain everything in good time... And Hyota, please feel free to continue your nap. We've had quite enough of your refreshing perspective."

"Thanks, I'm good. But don't worry, I'll keep my thoughts to myself," Mr. Bare-Legs replied, rejecting the suggestion from Sakiguchi, who was apparently tired of being interrupted—although he'd shared plenty of his refreshing perspective already.

The delinquent, meanwhile, was providing refreshment of a different sort in the form of another round of tea—as long as he kept his mouth shut, he came off like a genuine waiter.

Sakiguchi shrugged and continued.

"In our last encounter, we successfully—or rather, fortuitously—managed to drive back the Twenties, but I feared we would not be so lucky next time," he began. "To put the matter in extreme terms, even engaging with that woman and her organization would be a defeat of sorts—in this world, there are certain people with whom one should never get involved."

He sounded deadly serious.

And coming from the vice president of the Pretty Boy Detective Club, which everyone at school said you should never get involved with, those words bore all the more weight.

The fact is, he was probably right.

The last time I saw Rei, she'd hinted that our paths would cross again, but I couldn't think of anything I wanted more than to avoid such a reunion.

"And so I decided to request Sosaku's assistance in investigating her organization—its structure, its activities, its scale... The likelihood of crossing paths once more, and if we do, how to extricate ourselves from the situation... The two of us have been secretly looking into these matters."

They had?

True enough, that was work for the vice president of the Pretty Boy Detective Club, not the student council president. And just like last time, he'd gotten the child genius (and his formidable foundation) to help.

I couldn't help wondering why he hadn't called on the Yubiwa Foundation for help in investigating Kamikazari Middle School as well, but he seemed to keep the two completely separate in his mind.

His conscientious personality might've had something

to do with that, but it was also probably related to the odd relationships between the members of the Pretty Boy Detective Club, which is to say, the fact that when they weren't at HQ or doing club work, they refused to have anything to do with one another.

The club existed entirely thanks to its leader.

Sakiguchi and the child genius had no direct connection—even I could say that much.

"And? Did ya find anything out?" asked the delinquent, who was even more at odds with the student council president outside the art room than any of us (inside it, he was our waiter).

"We did," Sakiguchi nodded. "Simply put, the Twenties are, as you may recall, a delivery service—their business is to bring whatever they are asked to bring, be it people or goods, to the location where they are asked to bring it. They appear to have no political positions or ideology whatsoever."

"Hmmm. And yet, I sensed a certain faint aesthetic," Sotoin mused.

His standard for making such judgements was hard to grasp, but to tell the truth, I got what he was trying to say—after all, Rei could have treated us far worse when we were at her mercy.

It's true that they transported us like a bunch of parcels, but we were actually handled with a fair amount of care.

"Yes indeed. They certainly have standards, if not exactly an aesthetic—call it the pride that professional criminals take in their work. At the very least, I do not believe they will seek revenge on us. That should offer some sense of relief."

Interesting… So revenge was the thing he was most worried about, having run afoul of a criminal organization. A few superficial wins are no better than a loss if you have to spend the rest of your life watching your back— I'd assumed everything was over, and hadn't really been thinking about revenge, but I guess it was a pretty obvious concern.

Given how careful Sakiguchi had to be that his reputation wasn't ruined by the situation with his fiancée, I wasn't surprised he was on top of risk management—too bad for him he still couldn't rest easy when it came to the fiancée thing, though.

"As long as we proceed with caution, we will not cross paths with the Twenties again. I can guarantee you that much."

"…"

His statement was meant to be reassuring, but considering that the Pretty Boy Detective Club didn't know the first thing about proceeding with caution, that condition left me a little anxious.

Still, if that had been all he had to say, I would've taken it as good news, but Sakiguchi's expression remained dark.

"Well," he continued. "In the course of our investigation, we came across a piece of unexpected information, totally by accident—and that information made the whole situation infinitely more complex and suggestive."

"Suggestive, like Rei's figure?"

"Hyota. We're finished talking about Rei. She wasn't even included in the illustrations, now, was she?"

"Hmph. What's your problem? Just because you prefer a boyish figure—"

"If by boyish figure you are referring to the fiancée that my parents chose for me without my permission, then in the name of her honor, I would like to point out that her figure is not all that boyish—but as for the unexpected information, it had to do with Kamikazari Middle School."

"Kamikazari Middle School? Oho, and where might that be?"

The leader's eyes sparkled.

Does he have amnesia or something?

His curiosity must only have one channel—to put a positive spin on it, he's got an excellent capacity for concentrating on the matter at hand, but how could he have so quickly forgotten the name of the school where we'd just been conducting an undercover investigation?

And on top of that, our schools are neighbors!

But the leader's scatterbrained reaction was an

unexpected blessing, because it helped soften my own shock.

What on earth did the Twenties have to do with Kamikazari Middle School?

"We arrived at this information in the course of investigating the nature of the Twenties' activities. At the time, I couldn't believe my ears, but the source was a very reliable one—there is evidence that Fudatsuki, the school's current student council president, is engaged in business dealings with the Twenties."

"Business dealings…?"

A middle school student doing business with a criminal organization?

My first reaction was to blurt out that the very idea was ridiculous, but while Fudatsuki may be a middle school student, he's a middle school student who runs a casino in the school gym at night, along with a variety of other activities. Doing business with criminals might not be so surprising for a guy like him—in fact, even if it was total coincidence that his business partner was the Twenties, it actually seemed natural that he would be involved with an illegal organization.

"The Twenties being essentially a delivery service, they're acting as middleman in this situation—they seem to be making regular deliveries to Fudatsuki."

"He's m-meeting with her regularly…? That bastard, meeting with Rei?"

Mr. Bare-Legs seemed mysteriously jealous (honestly, "that bastard"?), but that aside—deliveries?

"You mean like the slot machines and poker tables? So that's how he got his hands on that stuff!"

"Yes, Michiru. I do believe the Twenties acted as middleman in those transactions as well—otherwise, it would be almost inconceivable for a middle school student to put together that kind of facility. That is not the essential point here, however—you see, a...private-sector company seems to be sending him consignments of products they have in development."

Hm?

For once, the skilled orator stumbled, and seemed for a moment to be at a loss for words... What was going on here?

The involvement of the Twenties, who were up to their elbows in illegal activity, was definitely a problem, but having business dealings with a private company didn't in and of itself seem like anything to get so worked up about.

"They appear to be paying Fudatsuki to beta test items under development—and it seems that the student council president's main source of income derives from reporting his impressions of the products he's tested."

"What the hell? That's his main source of income? So all he's gotta do is say if it was easy to use or not? Tell them whether he liked it or not?"

Sounds like one hell of a cushy job, the delinquent added sardonically.

"And that's how he's able to run the casino?"

"To the contrary, I'd say that's *why* he's running the casino—to test the product he's currently been commissioned to report on," Sakiguchi answered. "Those invisible black clothes Ms. Dojima told us about, the ones the kuroko was wearing."

24. Invisibility Wear

With that, all became clear.

That's how it felt, anyway, but it was just my imagination—there was still plenty I didn't know about the situation, though at least now I understood how Fudatsuki operated that casino.

Sakiguchi's words had pierced the heart of the matter.

It wasn't that he got the money to run the casino from his other "work," but that he ran the casino in order to do that work.

Yes, I do believe he was using the whole place for his own ends.

Using the eyes of the audience.

To test out those invisible black clothes.

To test them out… Or rather, to try them on for size.

He definitely wasn't using them to cheat his guests out of their money.

His customers were not the students of our neighboring school.

His customer was a corporation.

But—

"D-Does that kind of clothing really exist? I-I mean…
It's like something out of *Harry Potter*…"

Garments no one could see. No one but me.

It sounded too sci-fi to be real…

"I know. I could hardly believe it myself until I saw
it—that is, until I didn't see it. But when I heard your story the other day, Ms. Dojima, something clicked for me."

Even after investigating the matter with Sosaku, he
said, he didn't have a concrete idea of what the product
was.

"A man who vanished into thin air. I thought he must
have used the clothes to do that—and from your description, I was at least seventy-five percent sure that your
'Mr. Businessman' was my old acquaintance, the student
council president of Kamikazari Middle."

"…"

The pieces were falling into place.

That's why Sakiguchi had been so enthusiastic from
the start—when his two parallel investigations unexpectedly coalesced into one, he probably felt he'd had a stroke
of luck, even if he wasn't consciously trying to kill two
birds with one stone.

…And it had all panned out.

He'd unexpectedly been able to carry out an undercover investigation of Fudatsuki's illegal activities at

Kamikazari Middle, and—even more unexpectedly—been able to observe a test of the product Fudatsuki was reviewing, thanks to my eyesight.

To observe an invisible body.

Mayumi the Seer—?

"B-But… Any way you slice it, the development of a sci-fi product like that must be a trade secret, right?"

Even an ignorant middle schooler like me could well imagine that if a product like that got out into the world, an unimaginable sum of money would be at play—and that wasn't all. My mind naturally went to money first because this whole episode had started with a wad of counterfeit cash, but this went beyond money.

A product like that could change the world.

Just as airplanes had made the world smaller, and TVs had shaken it up, and cell phones had made it feel claustrophobic.

The world could be remade from the ground up.

This was the kind of thing that flipped common sense on its head—and very much not the kind of thing anyone should be entrusting to a middle school student.

A conservative, hard-headed adult should be in charge of this.

No matter how good Fudatsuki's head for business was—but what if the company had some other reason for asking him to do it?

Could something have necessitated them going

through a middle school student and an illegal organization like the Twenties—

"No upstanding citizen would take on the job."

A quiet yet clear voice—the child genius's voice.

Sosaku Yubiwa had spoken.

Not as an artist, but as a businessman involved in running a foundation.

"You see, the developers have every intention of putting it to an evil use."

25. The Arms Industry

An evil use.

What did he mean? Well, we probably weren't talking about cheating at cards.

Invisible black clothes—a cloak of invisibility.

There's no way something like that would be used for a heartwarming purpose like one of Doraemon's fantastical gadgets. Simply put, these clothes turned you into the Invisible Man, at which point you could probably carry out any crime imaginable.

I'm sure there would be plenty of demand for a product like that from above-board sectors of the economy, but in a surveillance society so overrun with security cameras, the demand from the underworld would surely be even greater.

A person who doesn't exist can't be caught, no matter what crime they commit—but even that was just the simple imaginings of a middle school student.

Without a doubt, the setting where this technology

would be most in demand and most likely to be used, even if it were illegal, was the battlefield.

Military application.

The very idea was horrifying, but if the Twenties were involved, then it wasn't so far-fetched—after all, the last time we'd gotten involved with Rei and her cronies, the case had involved military weaponry as well.

This company must be a regular client of theirs.

As a delivery service.

And even if it wasn't the same company as last time, the fact remained that the private-sector company Fudatsuki was involved with was a military contractor.

The arms industry… We were getting in deep.

An organization that wouldn't hesitate to flout the law.

"With that kind of backing, making some over-spec counterfeit bills would be a piece of cake—shit!"

The delinquent was really pissed.

"That asshole acts all full of himself, but he's just another dog at the feet of his masters. I'm as disappointed as I was when I realized that the saying 'dogs are man's best friend' really means that humanity's best friend isn't humanity."

The satire cut like a knife.

Apparently, he couldn't stand being sucked dry by a casino—and this casino in particular.

"I suspect Fudatsuki doesn't see himself as some

kind of subcontractor—he probably thinks he's playing hardball with this arms manufacturer. The two parties are certainly using each other; a two-way street, if you will. Having such a hefty pipeline to a company like that must have allowed him to expand his operations... But I hardly need point out that the situation is extremely dangerous."

Yes, it probably was dangerous.

In a sense, even more dangerous than a Lolita complex.

You definitely couldn't call Fudatsuki's business transparent.

After all, he wasn't the only one affected by his business dealings and economic activities.

Every one of the middle school students innocently trading chips back and forth in that dazzling casino was an unwitting party to his illegal activities—and that wasn't all.

The smallest misstep posed a huge risk.

Like how I'd unintentionally seen something I shouldn't have in the sky, and ended up getting kidnapped by the Twenties—an unexpected yet pre-ordained "unfortunate event" could befall those innocent boys and girls.

And not just the customers.

The Kamikazari students who'd signed on as bunny girls and dealers were at risk, too—they'd never get away with claiming it was just job training.

Of course, Fudatsuki's inner circle probably knew what was going on, but I couldn't imagine the entire staff did.

The casino itself probably violated Japanese law, but he'd stepped way over that line, and the next one as well.

No two ways about it, this operation went far beyond a "playful" or "boyish" spirit. If such things as right and wrong exist in this world, Fudatsuki's actions were clearly the latter.

"If clothes like that exist, they should just use them to sneak into the girls' locker room and call it a day," Mr. Bare-Legs muttered.

Um, no, that wouldn't be okay, either…

"So, Mr. President, whadda we do?"

Ignoring the comment from Mr. Bare-Legs, the delinquent darted a glance at the child genius, who had returned to his usual silent artiste routine, before turning to Sotoin for direction.

"Whaddaya think? Knowing you, I bet you see some kind of aesthetic beauty in what the Twenties are doing, and in Fudatsuki's casino—but even you've gotta admit they've gone too far, right?"

"Heh."

The president spread his hands in response to the delinquent's question.

"Michiru, if I'm not mistaken, you are asking if I think we should return to the Reasonable Doubt Casino and seek our revenge, seizing the right to run the business by beating the manager in another onstage showdown and smashing to smithereens the proving ground where he's been testing out those black clothes, before they can become a military weapon?"

Because in that case, my answer is yes, Sotoin continued. "Of course it is! Anything else would violate my personal aesthetic. To see the eye's delight and not pursue it is want of courage—ahem! Young Dojima! That is, Mayumi the Seer!"

"Y-Yes?"

I jumped a little to suddenly hear my name like that.

Manabu the Aesthete gave me an enthusiastic thumbs up.

"Rejoice. The time has arrived for you to offer up your eyesight in service to the greater good."

26. Once More Unto the Breach

It was hard for me to fully assess the plan that Sotoin elaborated for us because he spoke at such a lightning clip, but it seemed surprisingly well calculated—not that Sotoin calculates anything (after all, only his eye is trained, not his mind), but it was definitely true that we could achieve a great deal by putting the Reasonable Doubt Casino out of business.

We'd be depriving the guests of their night spot and the staff of their jobs, but we'd be protecting them at the same time—and we'd also be achieving our councilman's goal of taking preventive measures to protect the students of Yubiwa Academy.

It was too much to hope that we could totally sever the ties between Fudatsuki and the Twenties, which is to say his ties with the military contractor, but their dealings would probably take time to re-establish if we busted them up for the moment—and if we did so as invited guests of the casino, we'd be playing by their rules, even if those rules were illegal. Which is to say, there shouldn't be any lingering resentment that would come back to bite us.

And we had the means to do it, even if I wasn't wild about what they were.

With my eyesight, we'd be able to take care of the kuroko—which meant that breaking Fudatsuki's winning streak was more than an empty fantasy.

This was about as good as it could get for a plan thrown together without any forethought—but to implement it, we had to clear a number of hurdles.

Sotoin appeared bent on returning this very night to the Reasonable Doubt Casino... Which is to say, Kamikazari Middle School Gymnasium #2, but wouldn't that be kind of tricky?

I mean, we kind of stood out—after all, one of our party had been up on the stage only a few hours earlier.

If we showed up that very same night after having been thrown out in front of everyone, we were guaranteed to raise suspicions.

Not to mention the fact that Fudatsuki had referred to us as the members of the Pretty Boy Detective Club as he was seeing us out—although I guess it wasn't surprising that the student council president of Kamikazari Middle had done a bit of research about his putative rival school.

Setting aside whether he knew about the newbie

(me), we should probably assume that he'd recognized the other five from the start—and actually, it was quite possible he'd dropped that wad of cash in front of me precisely because he knew I was the newest member of the Pretty Boy Detective Club.

It was as though he'd targeted us first when he set out to expand his territory because we were most likely to get in his way—maybe I was being paranoid, but with a plot this tangled, it seemed entirely possible.

Wrapping up the whole affair before the casino closed that night seemed tough, but this was urgent—we definitely couldn't sit around waiting until it opened again a whole week later.

Nor could I imagine things cooling down if we did.

Another big problem was that we didn't have enough invitations—I'd only received a tenth of the original sum Fudatsuki dropped, which came to a hundred thousand yen.

Ten ten-thousand-yen bills, each with one invitation tucked inside—and we'd already used six of them.

That left four invitations.

In other words, we were two invitations short.

"I guess two of us could stay here…?" I timidly proposed.

Although I probably couldn't be one of those two, since Sotoin's plan relied on my eyesight.

That was my thought, but…

"I'm distressed that you would say such a thing, young Dojima," the leader chided. "Have you forgotten the fourth rule of the Pretty Boy Detective Club?"

The fourth rule—Be a team.

I hadn't forgotten, but now I realized that even though all the members were so freewheeling and independent, they apparently placed a lot of value on sticking together.

"B-But there just aren't enough invitations…"

"Fear not. I have an excellent plan."

The leader turned to the Pretty Boy Detective Club's resident artist.

"Sosaku. I'll be needing you."

As the child genius nodded silently, the nature of Sotoin's plan dawned on me—since copying the masters was the cornerstone of artistic skill, reproducing a couple of casino invitations would probably be child's play for someone like Sosaku Yubiwa.

Sotoin must want him to make two extras so that everybody had one—at least, that was my best guess.

I should have known that any excellent plan based on his excellent aesthetic wouldn't be nearly so logical.

27. Disguises

Fudatsuki's evil scheme had started with counterfeit bills, so I figured we would repay him by making counterfeit invitations, but Sotoin's plan was focused on the part of his evil scheme that involved the invisible kuroko—and we would repay him by becoming as invisible as the kuroko ourselves, and infiltrating the casino that way.

This explanation has probably left my readers quite confused, and indeed, I was quite confused myself, but perhaps thanks to his silent connection with Sotoin, the child genius sprang immediately into action—and while his face was blank, I suppose his heart may have been brimming with enthusiasm to carry out the leader's order.

I, however, was still in the dark.

"I see. In other words, you intend for us to melt into the scenery—in which case, we won't even need four invitations, let alone six."

It was only thanks to Sakiguchi's explanation (translation) that my dull mind finally grasped the whole plan.

"The staff entrance was around back," added the delinquent, who apparently had scoped out the layout on our last visit—although I'm not sure if he did so because he's thorough, or because he was considering possible escape routes after losing all his cash.

"The staff entrance? Huh? What do you mean?"

Mr. Bare-Legs seemed to be the only one who still didn't get it—which made sense, since I suppose he alone had some unresolved issues on the table.

The staff entrance.

In other words, Sotoin's plan wasn't for us to sneak into the Reasonable Doubt as guests, but to disguise ourselves as staff—after all, the art of disguise is a fundamental skill for detectives.

Be a detective.

The third rule of the Pretty Boy Detective Club.

We'd just fled the place in disgrace, and everyone knew our faces. We could go back in disguise, but even if we somehow fabricated two more invitations, if we went as guests the staff would probably be watching us like hawks.

And if they saw through our disguises, maneuvering would be that much harder—but if we went in as *staff*, well, that wasn't just a bold plan, it would hit them right in their blind spot.

We'd naturally be able to blend in, and as long as the other staff didn't recognize us, they wouldn't have their guard up—which meant we'd be free to carry out our sleuthing unhampered.

Plus, we wouldn't need invitations.

Well, it was true that we wouldn't need four, but we would need one. Even if five of us played back-up as staff members, someone had to face off with the maestro on stage.

The question was, who would it be—

"Ahem. I suppose it must be me."

The leader stepped forward.

…Part of me felt like this was insanely risky, but it also seemed like it might be our only option.

Sakiguchi had already been on stage, so he was out, and the delinquent specialized in losing, so he wouldn't do either—I could just imagine Michiru the Epicure being eaten alive.

Mr. Bare-Legs seemed more suited to physical activity and fooling around than an onstage showdown.

What about me, then? Well, I didn't even know the rules of the games, which meant I'd be more use assisting as "Mayumi the Seer."

The child genius seemed like he'd be able to apply his genius to gambling, but he and I couldn't communicate, which would render my assistance useless.

Which left Sotoin.

The leader himself would lead the attack.

Of course, he'd have to wear a disguise since they

already knew his face.

"Very true, young Dojima. Indeed, since all eyes will be on me, including those of the overseer sitting directly across from me, I'll probably need the most carefully constructed costume of all—hmm. Yes, that appears to be my only choice."

What does?

I found out soon enough.

And then we set off for Kamikazari Middle School once more.

28. The Only Choice

The members of the Pretty Boy Detective Club may have shone brightly in their somewhat formal dress, but I'd hardly say they blended into the shadows in the staff uniforms the child genius threw together so skillfully at the last minute.

Sakiguchi and the child genius were dealers, Mr. Bare-Legs was a security guard, and the delinquent was a bartender.

As for me, well, I was a bunny girl.

Seriously?

I was astounded that in the space of a month my gloomy old self had become stylish enough to pull off a bunny outfit, but the situation was unavoidable in at least two ways.

First, I'd already made one trip to the casino dressed as a boy—which meant that taking off my disguise paradoxically amounted to putting one on. Second, while the Reasonable Doubt did have some female dealers, I could hardly pretend to be one without knowing the rules—which left me with bunny girl (since security guard was clearly out of the question).

I'd joined the Pretty Boy Detective Club by dressing as a boy, and now I was disguising myself as a bunny girl, which was all topsy-turvy and left me with a confusing feeling, but the second reason was possibly even more important than the first.

If the leader was going on stage dressed as a girl, then as his subordinate, I couldn't very well complain about having to dress as one, too—yes.

Just as he'd done the last time we tangled with the Twenties, Sotoin was for a second time preparing to transform from a pretty boy into a pretty girl for the sake of his detective work.

Actually, the costume artist was so efficient at enabling his transformation that I couldn't help thinking this wasn't just the second time—in fact, he seemed to have a much harder time turning me into a bunny girl (sorry!).

Meanwhile, Mr. Bare-Legs was engaged in his own internal struggle—because naturally, the casino staff all wore long pants. Of course, he could expose his vaunted legs if he dressed as a bunny girl and skipped the stockings, which meant he was stuck with a choice: dress as a girl or wear long pants.

"D-Damn it… Give me the l-l-long pants…"

Is it really that big a deal?

From what I could tell, he hated the idea of dressing as a girl so much that he was willing to give up his identity—though I bet he'd look better than me in a bunny outfit.

"They call me 'he of the beautiful legs,' for chrissakes, I can't believe I'm covering them up… That'd be like Nagahiro, he of the underage beauties, silencing the voice he uses to manipulate young girls…"

"Who are you calling 'he of the underage beauties'? I will have it known that I do not use my voice for any such dubious purpose," Sakiguchi shot back in his beautiful voice.

Mr. Bare-Legs was so caught up with his own bare legs that he overlooked the competition from mine, exposed as they were by my bunny suit—a gross oversight, to be sure, but the fact that he didn't refuse to participate altogether suggested that even the guileless Mr. Bare-Legs (Mr. Long-Pants?) was conscious of his duties as a member of the Pretty Boy Detective Club.

Anyway, his vaunted legs did turn out to be indispensable for sneaking into the casino through the rear entrance to the gym, so I'm grateful he came along—a couple of guards were stationed by the back door, and it fell to Mr. Bare-Legs to lure them away.

Basically, he made a show of racing past the guards like some kind of suspicious character, and when they

followed him, we slipped into the gym in our disguises—
at which point he deftly dodged the doormen and joined
us inside before they could make it back to their posts.

"I'm so much slower in these damn pants..." he com-
plained dejectedly, but in any case, we made it in—meanwhile, Sotoin had come in through the front door and was
already seated at the blackjack table.

In that brilliantly lit room, the raving beauty's raving
beauty was almost overwhelming—it was as if it wasn't
the lights overhead that were shining, but Sotoin himself.

This time, he wasn't just dressed up, he was wearing
an actual dress.

"Hah. Our leader does indeed possess a special quality," Sakiguchi announced proudly.

Having pride in one's leader is a wonderful thing, but
if what had struck him was in fact the sight of a fifth grader
dressed up as a girl, then I couldn't help but conclude that
his condition had reached a level requiring serious professional intervention.

If we managed to clear up the problem with Fudatsuki, perhaps it was time for us to deal head-on with Sakiguchi's even more severe problem—anyway, it looked unnatural for so many staff members to be standing around
together, so we spread out through the casino to attend to
our various jobs.

I walked over to Sotoin.

...Come on, you weren't supposed to start gambling

until I could get here to appropriately (inappropriately?) assist you with my super eyesight!

Okay, I know you're not the delinquent, so you probably haven't burned through *all* your cash quite yet, but...

Silently, I counted the chips next to him, and was surprised to find he'd already amassed quite a pile.

Even though I'm pretty sure he started out with as little seed money as possible to create the impression of an even bigger win, he'd racked up that much in half an hour...?

Earlier, when he'd come as a pretty boy, he'd played beautifully, but I couldn't imagine turning into a pretty girl had done much to improve his game. More likely, he was simply winning because he had a goal this time—that is, a reason to win.

In the time it took me to think those thoughts, his pile grew even larger.

At this rate, he wouldn't even need my help until he got on stage... But I was just one of five infiltrating the casino in disguise.

If any of us were discovered, the rest would fall like dominoes—which meant I couldn't just hang around doing nothing.

Plus, in my case, being exposed meant not only having the world know I was a spy but also that I'd dressed up as a bunny girl, which gave me extra reason to play my role to the hilt. I couldn't really overdo it—although in a sense I already was.

So I started sending Sotoin signals as we'd agreed in advance—looking right through the cards the dealer was handing out.

I'd had my glasses off from the start.

…Now that I was actually doing it, the degree to which I was breaking the rules was glaringly clear. If everyone could peek at cards like this, casinos couldn't exist—which made me even more conscious of how unforgivable the secret actions of the kuroko on stage were.

An eye for an eye.

I couldn't imagine a more fitting situation for that saying—but all the same, I was keeping the signs I sent Sotoin to the bare minimum.

It's not that I'd lost my nerve or was feeling guilty or anything, but I was afraid that since I didn't know the rules, I'd make a mistake if things got too complicated.

My real job would start with the special program, when the kuroko showed up—and going too crazy now would be putting the cart before the horse.

Watching so closely made me uneasy about Sotoin's betting strategy—he went all in every time. Yet somehow he still didn't get wiped out. It was weird.

Maybe he just knew how to come through in the clutch?

Even so, I couldn't help feeling uneasy—his way of winning had a certain je ne sais quoi, and, as a girl, Sotoin was so gorgeous that he was attracting quite an audience.

I felt like everyone was looking at my bunny outfit, which made me wildly embarrassed, but actually, no one was paying me any mind—which was fairly humiliating in itself, but anyway, I was worried that the more people looked at us, the higher the chance we'd be discovered.

On the other side of the hall, meanwhile, a hubbub was developing around the incredibly delicious free drinks—apparently the bartender was going a little overboard.

And the child genius was taking to his role as dealer at the poker table by displaying a mysterious degree of sociability—which I could only hope he would one day direct my way.

Sakiguchi wasn't making the same effort, but he nevertheless seemed quite popular with the ladies—I'd been worried he was at the greatest risk of exposure since he'd already been up on stage, but maybe because he was so used to hiding the age of his fiancée, he appeared to be the most fastidious of us all. I still felt nervous, though.

For his part, Mr. Bare-Legs was just standing around like a wet rag.

The pants must have sucked up all his energy—that's how gloomy he looked. He'd fit in better at a funeral parlor than an amusement parlor.

Which was why, when I finally heard someone say "Congratulations!" to Sotoin, sitting there with his overflowing pile of chips, I breathed a sigh of relief.

"You've won the right to participate in the special program!"

"I have?"

The pretty girl was beaming.

29. Showdown

With that, the second show of the night began—a show-down between the challenger and the overseer, who was betting the right to run his casino.

A dressed-up Sotoin faced Fudatsuki on stage—while the same bunny girl as before grabbed the mic and began explaining just how extraordinary it was for two such shows to take place in one night.

The audience swelled with excitement at her skilled performance—though she'd been cold to me, her fellow bunny girl.

She'd made such a fuss over me when I was dressed as a boy, and now… Well, that was just fine by me.

It would've been big trouble if anyone had seen through my disguise.

In that sense, we'd already scored a huge success by getting to the showdown before I'd had occasion to inter-act with Fudatsuki.

Thanks to the costume artist, my appearance had

been utterly transformed, but (unlike Nagahiro the Orator) I couldn't alter my voice, so the second I exchanged words with him, he would have known who I was.

Now all I had to do was watch from the floor to see what Fudatsuki's invisible assistant did during the game, and signal to Sotoin what to do about it—which didn't sound all that easy, but just being aware of the kuroko, who they all thought no one could see, gave us a big advantage. Now if we could only figure out how to capitalize on the fact that they hadn't yet noticed that we'd noticed...

"Should be an easy win from here on out," the delinquent whispered as we passed each other. "And by the way, I put all the money I took out of the ATM on the leader."

"..."

Don't make this any more complicated than it already is!

Now I had to use my eyesight to make sure the delinquent didn't fall further into financial ruin, too—the pressure was growing.

For the main event, the challenger—Sotoin—chose blackjack.

Was that the only game he knew how to play?

"No, my guess is that the leader has thought up a plan of his own—after all, looking over someone's shoulder in blackjack is pointless, which means the invisible kuroko's help won't be as useful as it was in poker," Sakiguchi noted.

Setting aside the question of whether the leader actually thought about anything, Sakiguchi's point made sense—although he'd apparently failed in his scheme to get the child genius up on stage as the dealer.

This time, there was no dealer.

"..."

Mr. Bare-Legs, meanwhile, looked like he was barely hanging on. We had to wrap this up fast so Mr. Bare-Legs could bare his legs again!

"And with that, let the games begin!" the bunny girl announced, before exiting the stage—my eyes were peeled, watching for the appearance of the kuroko.

Everything was going to be fine.

Considering the situation, I bore a heavy responsibility, but I'd practiced plenty of scenarios in the art room (while Sotoin was getting done up as a girl) so I'd be ready no matter what happened—whatever that kuroko did, I'd show him who was boss.

Since this was my first real mission as a member of the Pretty Boy Detective Club, I was going to knock their socks off—or so I thought.

But instead, an unexpected twist appeared in the plot.

Or rather.

Didn't appear.

30. Invisible

"...?"

Nearly thirty minutes had passed since the blackjack game between Fudatsuki (in formal dress) and Sotoin (in a dress) began—yet the kuroko still hadn't appeared on stage.

The only two people on stage were the players—and no matter how hard I looked, I couldn't see a third party trying to interfere.

Wait, no, don't panic, I told myself—because if I got upset, I wouldn't be able to see what I needed to see.

But my eyesight isn't like that. I can't arbitrarily switch it from on to off or high to low—since my brain can't control it, I even see things I'm not trying to see, and things I don't want to see.

Which meant that if anyone else was on stage, I should have been able to see them whether I wanted to or not—so what was going on?

Was the kuroko still lurking in the wings?

Waiting for some kind of cue?

But…how could they be so blasé about this? For Fudatsuki, everything was at stake. This was hardly the time to keep an ace up his sleeve, to display his "playful spirit"—plus, with the whole audience watching, now seemed the perfect moment to test out the invisibility suit.

I mean, if he didn't test it out now, you could almost accuse him of falling down on the job.

"…What's the matter, Ms. Dojima?" Sakiguchi asked in a concerned tone, sauntering over to my side like one employee chatting idly to another.

It was rough to have the guy with the worrisome dating preferences worrying about me, but I managed to hiss back, "I-I think they might have caught on!"—referring, of course, to my eyesight, and not his dating preferences.

"Indeed, Fudatsuki may not be using the kuroko at present because he fears we will see through his scam…"

Did that mean he'd been wise to our disguises from the start? Here we thought we were being so sly, but maybe he'd merely been doling out rope for us to hang ourselves with.

In that case, Sotoin on stage in his dress, Mr. Bare-Legs in the long pants he hated so much, and most of all me in my bunny outfit, were all truly disgracing ourselves—we were already swinging from the gallows.

"Hmm… You know, this could actually be a positive

development. If Fudatsuki doesn't use his dirty tricks, then our leader will be able to take him on fair and square…"

That was one way of looking at it, I suppose (if you weren't wearing a bunny outfit, that is).

If I used my eyesight to boot, the match wouldn't just be fair, it would be tilted in Sotoin's favor, but that would probably violate the leader's aesthetic.

It sounds weird, but I felt like we could only play dirty if our opponent did us the favor of playing dirty too—as long as I didn't see the kuroko, I couldn't signal Sotoin about Fudatsuki's cards.

Which meant the outcome of this game rested entirely on luck.

A fair fight.

"Wonder how this'll play out. There's a sort of flow to gambling, ya know…"

Was the weak player saying something?

Flow, huh? The only thing that flows is your money, out of your wallet.

Anyway, it was too soon to tell—Fudatsuki might still be getting the lay of the land, and the kuroko could appear at any moment.

I watched the game unfold, unable to squelch my anxiety—the audience was even more excited than when Sakiguchi had been on stage, but I felt even less able to share in the mood.

Wishing I could sooth my unease even a little, I watched the game more attentively than all the guests who'd staked their cash on it—although aggressively might be a better word than attentively. In any case, my emotions had no effect whatsoever on my eyesight.

I couldn't see what couldn't be seen.

But even though I didn't know the rules, scrutinizing the game this seriously did give me a sense of how the match was playing out—and it was an exquisite back-and-forth.

Almost as if they were following a script.

A tug of war seemingly directed by an unseen hand.

As exciting as if it had been made to order for the audience—

"You really don't see anything, Ms. Dojima?" Sakiguchi asked.

Repeating the question could not turn the invisible visible—and yet, the arc of the game seemed impossible without the involvement of the kuroko.

What was going on?

I could think of only one answer—the kuroko was on stage, *but was somehow invisible even to me.*

"..."

As my thoughts became more and more confused, I kept trying to think—to deduce.

Could the kuroko's black clothes have been upgraded in the space of just a few hours? Or perhaps my eyes had just gotten tired? Up till now my eyes had felt like nothing more than an obstacle to my dreams, but now I feared more than anything in the world that they'd given out on me.

Just when I finally thought I'd be able to use my eyesight for a just cause—or if not just, at least beautiful—things had taken this terrible turn.

Calm down. Calm down.

If Fudatsuki was one step ahead of us and *had* figured out a way to somehow undermine our investigation, what could it possibly be?

"I don't like the look of this... I'm certain Fudatsuki is biding his time, planning to snatch back all the chips at the last second," muttered Sakiguchi, who had fallen into just such a trap himself. But he didn't seem to have a plan to get around it—and it goes without saying that the delinquent didn't either.

As for Mr. Bare-Legs, by this point he was completely useless.

Mr. Bare-Legs without his bare legs was as ineffective as me without my special eyesight.

What was Fudatsuki doing?

How had he managed to evade my eyes?

How...

"Hahaha!"

Just as I was about to hang my head in frustrated despair—that is, just as I was about to give up on looking, it happened.

As I went to turn my eyes from the stage like I'd turned them away from the sky, that loud laugh rang out—loud enough that it echoed across the hall, silencing the raucous crowd.

Needless to say, it came from Sotoin.

Given the hearty belly laugh coming from the seemingly delicate, elegant girl on the stage, it was no surprise that the audience fell silent as if they'd been doused with ice water, but Sotoin himself appeared not to care in the least.

To the contrary, he—or rather she—continued laughing loudly.

"…What do you find so amusing?"

Fudatsuki must have been upset that his opponent had turned the excited mood of the audience sour just like that, but apparently he still felt he had to play the attentive manager.

"Oh, nothing. It's just that I find myself in a tight spot! And since a fellow like me shines most beautifully in just such moments, I couldn't help but be stunned by my own radiance!"

"…"

Fudatsuki's expression tensed at this mystifying speech, topped off by the beautiful girl across the table referring to herself as a "fellow"—but he was still the president of the student council, and a businessman, and a con artist to boot.

"You seem to have quite the passion for beauty," he countered—putting on a supremely relaxed front.

Although he was probably the one who felt stunned.

I ground my teeth in frustration at being able to see his face so clearly, but nothing more.

"But, young lady, if you let superficial beauty distract you completely, you're sure to lose your footing. Saint-Exupéry wrote, 'What is essential is invisible to the eye'— and the same holds for beauty, I am sure."

Real beauty is as invisible as air, he pronounced shamelessly.

But at his words, the audience erupted once again— Sotoin, who had enjoyed the audience's favor as a beautiful girl, had managed to turn even them against him.

But she, which is to say he, seemed completely undaunted by that fact.

"I will never lose my footing. To the contrary, it is feet, or rather legs, that are so often my salvation. I'm familiar with Saint-Exupéry myself, you see, and have read that beautiful passage quite carefully. The words on the page did indeed say that what is essential is invisible to the eye. I was most impressed by them."

"…"

"Yet nothing truly beautiful is invisible to a fellow like me—be it on the outside or the inside, the written word or the air itself, I am sure to see it. No matter how blinding, I never turn my eyes away from that which glitters!"

And he wasn't done.

"My dear Fudatsuki, if even your lies are beautiful, then I will do you the service of bearing witness to them in all their glory!"

It was quite a declaration—of war.

Naturally, the audience did not erupt as before—though the sound of four pairs of hands clapping brazenly did echo through the gymnasium.

I knew who they belonged to without needing to look.

It was like we were being shown a beauty that did not collapse under the pressure of the atmosphere, the *air*, in the hall—but that only served to make the situation more dangerous than it had been a few moments earlier.

Worst-case scenario, if Sotoin had ended up losing, we could have returned the following week to try some other strategy, but now that option was totally kaput— Sotoin and the four boys who had clapped for him would definitely be banned from the casino.

We had to finish this thing here and now.

In the face of such a challenging challenger, Fudatsuki abandoned his polite front and simply glared silently at the pretty girl as they played—apparently, he was done with fun and games, and was just as intent on settling the matter as we were.

Dammit.

Think. Think. Thinkthinkthinkthinkthink!

Fudatsuki's words left no question in my mind that he was somehow using the invisibility suit—using it to control the flow of the match.

But why couldn't I see anything?

What was I overlooking?

What could I see—and what could I not see?

A moment ago, when I could no longer stand the pressure and had started to turn my eyes away from the stage, they'd been pulled back by Sotoin's voice—by his aesthetic… Come to think of it, I'm the kind of person who turns her eyes away from a lot of things.

What did I need to face?

I knew the answer already: myself.

The thing I needed to look at was myself. That's why I'd joined the Pretty Boy Detective Club, because I wanted to work alongside a leader who'd said my eyes were beautiful.

Mayumi the Seer, she of the beautiful eyes. He'd called me that. Was that who I was?

Yes, in part—that might be my strength, maybe even my beauty, but it was also my weakness, my fault, the source of my feelings of inferiority.

Then what were my other weaknesses and faults? What else did I feel inferior about?

The self I didn't want to see…

The self I ignored like empty air.

"…"

I faced myself in my bunny suit. What the hell was I doing? But that didn't matter right now—if I took a step back, it wasn't that weird to be wearing a bunny suit in a casino. It was like wearing a swimsuit at the pool. That didn't change even if I looked at the situation with my too-good eyes—so what *was* weird about this situation?

It was obvious.

The fact that here I was in a casino even though I knew essentially nothing about the rules of the games. Not poker, not roulette, not baccarat, not the slot machines—and not even blackjack. I didn't know any of the rules.

Now *that* was extremely weird.

From an objective perspective, I was so out of place that I had to ask myself what the hell I was doing there. But I hadn't—I hadn't faced up to that part of myself.

I hadn't even made an attempt to learn the rules.

Even if Sotoin hadn't banned me from playing, I'm sure I would have messed around for a few minutes and then given up, telling myself it was boring.

But it was only boring because I was illiterate when it came to gambling—just like you can't watch some movies without a certain level of education, and you can't enjoy some novels without knowing the context, and you can't understand some works of modern art unless you see them with your own eyes.

Certain scenes can't be seen without the right knowledge.

Certain things can't be seen even if they're in plain sight.

Just like you wouldn't realize you were surrounded by air unless you knew air existed—yes, it was that simple.

What if the problem wasn't that I wasn't seeing it?

What if I *was* seeing it, but not realizing I was—

"Sakiguchi, this might be a stupid question, but…"

If someone had informed Fudatsuki about the bunny girl who had been helping Sotoin at the blackjack table earlier—if he had found out about my eyesight at that point, found out who I really was, then naturally he would've also found out how faltering my attempts at assistance had been, and how little I knew about the game.

And if he knew who I was, well then, I guess our little game of Othello in the lounge had shown him just how little I knew about games in general.

So to get around the too-good eyesight of an ignorant girl, all he had to do was use a strategy so obvious that anyone else in the place would have seen it immediately—

"Is there a rule in blackjack that says the dealer gets to trade in cards in the middle of the game, but the other players don't?"

31. The Reveal

The trick, once it dawned on me, was infuriatingly sim-ple—and the scam infuriatingly transparent.

The unseen kuroko.

The invisibility suit.

Since it'd had such a big impact on me and been such an effective racket, I'd made the mistake of assuming that it was the only way the technology could be applied—but if this was really the latest, most cutting-edge scientific technology, then logically it should be adaptable to more than just clothing.

For instance, there ought to be zillions of military ap-plications other than uniforms—from guns to knives to bullets to missiles to tanks to fighter jets.

This was the kind of stealth technology that could be used for anything.

According to the information Sakiguchi had gathered in advance, the secret business dealings going on at Kami-kazari Middle definitely weren't limited to clothes—and the technology could be applied just as easily to cards.

Trick cards *that were invisible when face down, but visible when face up*—that is, cards that only appeared when they were turned over on the table.

An entirely harmless item if you used it to perform magic tricks, and an entirely crooked one if you used it for gambling.

It worked exactly like a card tucked up your sleeve. You'd need some skill to mix the invisible cards in with your hand or trade them out while everyone was watching, but I've got to say, the fact that you could do so surreptitiously was exceedingly unfair.

Worst of all, Fudatsuki had brazenly used the trick knowing full well that I could see what he was doing. He'd made a fool of me, and I couldn't hide my mortification—but the truth was, I *had* been a fool.

Such a fool I couldn't even complain about being made a fool of.

It was unbelievable, I hadn't noticed his foul play even though he'd been doing it since the very first round—I'd simply assumed there must be some rule stating that Fudatsuki, the dealer, always got to have one more card in his hand than his opponent, Sotoin, and moreover that he could decide whether to count it or not at the end of the round.

I'd been looking without seeing.

But once I did see, I no longer needed to hold back—I

could hurl every bit of anger I felt straight at him.

Being made a fool of for being ignorant enough to tag along to a casino without knowing any of the rules may have been inevitable, but just because it was inevitable didn't mean my anger would magically disappear.

I have a hot temper for someone so gloomy.

That's another personality flaw I've got to deal with—but now wasn't so much the time to deal with it as to bludgeon the dealer with it.

I aimed the hammer of my anger at Fudatsuki up on the stage.

Unforgivable!

My eyes glittered.

32. Epilogue

Monday morning.

I headed to school half awake, hardly having slept—which made the events of the night before feel a bit dreamlike.

And in fact, they already belonged to a dream world.

That previous night was the last time the Reasonable Doubt Casino would ever open its doors—as Sotoin had announced after putting an end to Fudatsuki's lucky streak and brilliantly seizing the right to run his casino.

"My friends, the fun and games are over. Please exit beautifully," he pronounced from the epicenter of enemy territory, having claimed victory in what you might call the ultimate away game. Personally, I was shivering at the possibility that either the audience or staff might riot, but everyone took his (her) announcement that the venue was closing with surprising calm.

I guess they knew it was coming.

The defeat of the charismatic maestro equaled the

end of everything—and indeed it was so.

Even as a first-time guest, I could tell at a glance that no one would be able to fill his shoes.

Or maybe they were just impressed by how Sotoin won.

In my rage, I signaled the suit and value of every card I saw to him, but he didn't use that information to torture his opponent.

Instead, he quickly and cleanly brought the game to a close.

I doubt he possessed the subtlety to manipulate the flow of the game and get the audience riled up in the first place, but one thing I can say is that Sotoin didn't humiliate the student council president of Kamikazari Middle School—and while I'm sure Fudatsuki's pride was hurt all the same, the wound was as slight as it could have been.

Was that part of Sotoin's aesthetic as well?

If so, then his generosity of spirit was immeasurably greater than my own, considering I'd abandoned myself completely to anger—but in any case, we managed to escape that "nest of vipers," as the delinquent had called it, without any casualties (on the way home, Mr. Bare-Legs did violently tear off the pants that the child genius had sewn for him, but that's another story).

For the record, the delinquent—who had demonstrated his trust in the leader by betting every yen on him that he'd taken out of an ATM on the way there—

managed to win back everything he'd lost on our first visit and somehow come out even, which may be another sign of the leader's skill in watching out for his subordinates.

Anyway—the next morning.

Monday.

I shook off my sleepiness, slipped out of my bunny suit and into my boy's uniform, and headed to school—with my glasses on, of course.

By that point I was completely confused as to what I ought to be wearing, but at the very least, I knew my glasses were indispensable if I wanted every day to be everyday.

Since I'd used my eyes a bit too much the night before, the spot behind them was aching, but it wouldn't last long—and anyway, my head probably hurt more.

Because even though we'd shut down the Reasonable Doubt Casino more or less according to plan, it wasn't like everything was neatly resolved.

We'd prevented Fudatsuki from invading Yubiwa Academy's territory or hooking our student body on the poisonous delights of gambling—but his economic activities were by no means limited to the casino.

We'd also succeeded in ending his tests, and now that word was out about a person with eyesight like mine, the company might have to start over from scratch in developing their invisibility suit—or their invisibility technology in general.

But we hadn't severed the ties between Kamikazari Middle School and the Twenties—which meant the root of the problem still remained.

Both as student council president of Yubiwa Academy and vice president of the Pretty Boy Detective Club, Sakiguchi would no doubt continue to harbor a level of anxiety about this issue that equaled my anxiety about the age of his fiancée.

"Don't look so down, Nagahiro. There's more to see from that swindler. I'm certain another splendid showdown lies in store for us."

The all-important club president was as light-hearted as always—but by "more to see," did he mean Fudatsuki had beautiful aspects?

That scam artist?

Well… Regardless of what else there may or may not have been to see, now that he mentioned it, and now that the case was over, I realized Fudatsuki wasn't driven simply by business and horse-trading and product tests after all.

I'd been so pissed off the other day that I hadn't noticed—but he did have his own sort of line in the sand.

Perhaps it was only visible to him—perhaps the truth was that not Sotoin and not even I could see it—but looking back on recent events with a cool head, it seemed to me that while we'd implemented practically the only strategy available to us, Fudatsuki'd had plenty of options on the table.

And targeting my knowledge—or rather, lack there-of—was probably one of the riskier ones.

It was perfectly likely that I would go ahead and use my own dirty trick whether or not I realized he was using his invisible card scam.

He could instead have taken a firm stand and refused to bring Sotoin up on stage no matter how much he won, or he could have kicked the fake bunny girl (me) out of the casino.

And those were just the ones I came up with off the top of my head.

Instead, he chose a challenge and incited an incident.

Yes, I do believe this affair was the product of a playful spirit after all.

But if Fudatsuki got involved with the Twenties and even tangled with a private military contractor for the sake of amusement, then far from being reassured, I felt the situation was dicier than ever… For now, however, there was nothing more I could do.

Well, there was one thing—I might as well start by learning the rules of blackjack.

As I walked toward school mulling all of this over, I spotted an unfamiliar figure in a school uniform—a Kamikazari uniform. Well, speak of the devil (or at least, the middle schooler).

No way, could the next wave of the invasion be

starting already? I was immediately on my guard, but the boy greeted me amiably.

"Top of the morning, Mayumi Dojima."

I recognized that voice.

"It's me. Here," he swept his bangs back from his fore-head—yes, it was Fudatsuki.

Seeing him in a school uniform after only having seen him in a suit or a tuxedo was weird, to say the least, but I recognized one thing about him for sure—that reassuring smile, which is to say, that swindler's smile.

Come to think of it, we were in almost exactly the same spot where I'd picked up the million yen—which couldn't be a coincidence.

He'd been lying in wait for me.

… And not only that, he knew my name even though I'd never told it to him.

"Don't worry. I haven't come here for revenge—the damage you and your associates did to me was far greater than you might imagine. We'll be good boys and girls until things cool off—please tell that to Sakiguchi."

"O-Okay…"

Dressed in his school uniform, he looked more like the boy he was—but I couldn't let my guard down. He wasn't the type to actually behave well just because he said he was going to be a good boy.

And once those doubts set in, the part about not coming for revenge and the damage being so severe started to sound suspicious, too. But even if it was true, he and his associates might already be laying the groundwork for a comeback.

"S-So… Why're you here?" I asked timidly. I figured this might be my only chance to drop the formal language.

"To deliver a love letter. Not from me, of course. From one of our bunny girls."

Ohhhhh, that bunny girl.

She sure was pushy—first the phone number, now a love letter.

"I won't tell her you're a girl, so please, give her a call—she worked hard for me at the casino. And by the way, she was the one in the kuroko outfit last night."

Interesting… She must have been busy, with two jobs to keep on top of.

Anyway, he didn't have to keep my gender a secret. I'd rather he told her, actually. My life is complicated enough already.

But when the student council president himself handed me the letter with a heart drawn across the flap, I felt like I had to take it.

Crap, now what do I do…

"Oh, and not just Sakiguchi—please give my regards to the pretty girl who lectured me on aesthetics as well. Consider this a flirtatious reply. I don't intend to exact revenge, but tell her I'd love to go around again someday."

I had a feeling his "flirtatious reply" might be the real

reason he was here—it sent a shiver down my spine, like the proverbial dagger hidden behind a smile, but it also suggested that whatever he knew about my real identity or the existence of the Pretty Boy Detective Club, he hadn't yet figured out who Sotoin was.

Which made sense, since he was still in fifth grade.

If Fudatsuki investigated Yubiwa Academy for the purposes of an inter-school turf war, Sotoin's name wouldn't come up—so despite the weirdness of the student council president of Kamikazari Middle flirting with a fifth-grade boy in drag, I breathed a sigh of relief.

"Speaking of which," I asked. "I never did get your full name—I'll pass on your messages, so do you mind telling me?"

"Lai. Lai Fudatsuki. That's L-a-i, not L-i-e. Please, don't hesitate to call on me if you ever have a problem, and don't think twice about the division between our schools—I'm always ready to consult, especially if it's about money."

"O-Okay. Consult, huh."

"Take off those colored glasses, and you may find I'm not such a bad guy after all. Anyhow, it's up to you," he said, and turned on his heel.

I didn't have a reason to stop him, and if he was leaving then I guess we didn't have anything else to discuss, but still, I felt like I had some lingering questions, so I reflexively called out, "W-Wait," and chased after him.

I didn't know what I'd say when I caught up to him—but fortunately, I never did.

Because when I followed him around the corner, I stopped short—it was a long, straight road without any side streets to turn down, yet he was nowhere to be seen.

"…Okay, okay."

Had I seriously fallen into the same trap again? He was a real one-trick pony.

I took off my (non-colored) glasses and scanned my surroundings to see if I could spot Fudatsuki in an invisibility suit—but…

"Huh?"

No matter how hard I looked, nothing changed—I scoured the scene in every direction, but Fudatsuki failed to appear.

Like a scam—like the air itself.

Lai Fudatsuki had vanished completely.

"…"

What is essential is invisible to the eye.

What if the "essential" thing Fudatsuki was referring to when he so shamelessly quoted Saint-Exupéry wasn't his transparently obvious invisible cards, but his ultimate trump card? Apparently, he'd managed to bring the show to a close without revealing his strongest suit, even to me.

If so, then this hadn't even amounted to a preliminary skirmish—and it made sense that he wasn't thinking about revenge: he didn't think he'd lost.

The showdown between beauty and fraud, between a boyish spirit and a playful one.

The real struggle between the detective club and the maestro—was yet to come.

And yet, I still wasn't at all sure whether a person like me, who couldn't even see her own *self* clearly, could bear witness to that battle—I can only wrap things up by saying, it's opaque to me.

Afterword

The saying that things go well about a fifth of the time is by no means limited to gambling, but is supposed to be the most fitting ratio for anything a person might get absorbed in. Succeeding twenty percent of the time gives you just about the perfect sense of achievement, doesn't it? If you came out on top ninety percent of the time, I think you'd eventually get bored and wouldn't want to keep on going. Perhaps you could say that a certain randomness is needed to keep things from becoming routine. I suppose it's like this: Even if we all need a little excitement in our day-to-day lives, life would be pretty trying if *every* day were exciting, and so having an eventful day every one out of five or so makes for the best balance. Probability theory is fairly absolute, and it would be silly to expect any change on that front, but that's precisely why the pleasure of achieving something with a low probability is itself so absolute. That human beings gravitate toward things with a low probability of success rather than a high one suggests that we're not necessarily controlled by the simple desire to succeed; instead, it seems to me we seek out challenges with a low probability of success, which is to say a high level of difficulty, because overcoming them tends to bring greater joy. But if you think about it, this means that people blessed with fabulous luck, for whom success comes four out of five times and all of life is smooth sailing—that is, for whom life is impossibly good—must also find life impossibly boring. I'm pretty sure that's not the case, but I do suspect that those people wish that now and then something wouldn't go their way. After all, I believe there's something in all of us that wants to go up against ridiculous odds, fail, and say, "Well, there you go."

And so this has been the second story in the *Pretty Boy* series. What a name for a series. These events take place just after the previous volume, *Pretty Boy Detective Club: The Dark Star that Shines for You Alone.* Unlike most of the characters in the other novels I've written, the members of this club are actually capable of acting as a group, which makes writing this series something of a fresh experience for me. So there you have it, volume two of the *Pretty Boy* series: *The Swindler, the Vanishing Man, and the Pretty Boys.*

Kinako, who did the cover for volume one, has been kind enough to do the art for this one as well, giving us a very beautiful picture of Michiru the Epicure and Nagahiro the Orator. Thank you very much, Kinako. This book is my second for Kodansha's new Taiga imprint, and volume three should be on its way before long. I hope you'll read that one too.

NISIOISIN

Prolific and palindromic NISIOISIN won the 2002 Mephisto Prize at the age of only twenty for his debut mystery novel *Decapitation: Kubikiri Cycle*. Since then he has penned more than one hundred novels across numerous series, in addition to many comics and television scripts. He is one of the best-selling Japanese authors in recent memory, and has been hailed for breaking down the barriers between mainstream literary fiction and so-called light novels.

Seraph of the End

Guren Ichinose: Catastrophe at Sixteen

Story by Takaya Kagami
Art by Yamato Yamamoto

All 4 Volumes Available Now

The apocalypse is not only near, but a certainty. Set before the event and the aftermath detailed by the hit manga, this stand-alone prequel light novel series chronicles the inexorable approach of the reign of vampires. At the center of this story arc are the trials of Guren Ichinose, who enters an academy for the insufferably privileged and hides his true strength even as he is trampled on.

And Don't Miss...

Guren Ichinose: Resurrection at Nineteen

Story by Takaya Kagami
Art by Yo Asami
Volumes 1-2 Available Now!